An Amish Widow's Window

Amanda Roxley

Published by Trellis Publishing, 2021.

This is a work of fiction. Similarities to real people, places, or events are entirely coincidental.

AN AMISH WIDOW'S WINDOW

First edition. July 16, 2021.

Copyright © 2021 Amanda Roxley.

ISBN: 979-8224356539

Written by Amanda Roxley.

AN AMISH WIDOW'S WINDOW

AMANDA ROXLEY

An Amish Widow's Window

Amanda Roxley

Chapter 1: Flashbacks

Falling in love can happen all at once and also over a long period of time. Some people say that there is only one moment, and in that moment, you know that you've fallen in love. Falling in love, for Elizabeth, happened more or less, by accident. Elizabeth Brenneman fell in love suddenly yet slowly at the same time. His name was James Harper. She was sitting inside the Neptune Diner on the corner of Pine and Orange Streets with some of her new English girlfriends when James Harper arrived on the scene. James was the boyfriend of Megan Sanchez, a short plumpy Latino girl, with thick dark brown girls. She was also endowed with a generous chest, an amazing smile, and a silly laugh. When James came to the diner at 1 am in the morning and sat down by Megan, Elizabeth liked him immediately, but never thought she would fall in love with James. Why?

·James was Megan's boyfriend,

·James was an Englishman.

·She was/is(?) Amish.

·Elizabeth was an honest girl.

·James was wrong for Elizabeth in every way.

·James had a huge tattoo on his left shoulder (and Elizabeth didn't care for the Englishmen's tattoos.)

Elizabeth loved the Lord, and she never wanted to fall into a path that led to dishonesty, cheating, or leaving her family. She didn't cheat, actually, but it felt like it. While Elizabeth was experiencing Rumspringa, a time when Amish youth are allowed to enter the "modern world" and decide if they want to remain Amish, she found herself taking a liking to the English dance styles. Every Friday night

Elizabeth and her new English friends would go to a local Christian church hall and take part in something called contra dancing. Contra dancing occurred in a square formation, but you also danced with your partner and up and down the hall in lines with another set of partners simultaneously. In fact, it was quite difficult to explain what contra was or why she loved it, but she did, nonetheless. Elizabeth wasn't quite used to dancing with so many people, but it was fun, and she loved the music. There was an array of sounds that filled the air; delicate, yet elaborate wooden instruments with strings produced a sound that she had never heard before. The people dressed in long, flowy skirts, in bright oranges, blues, pinks, and even reds, as they danced across the hall with a grace that she longed to achieve.

Although Elizabeth usually arrived without a date to the local Friday night contra dancing, one night Megan said she could not go dancing and it wasn't a problem if she went with James. Elizabeth considered what a quandary that put her in...if she was in her Amish community this would never happen. Of course, a lot of things would never happen, such as dancing, going out on a Friday night, or drinking a milkshake at 1 am at the local diner. She loved all of it and hated all of it at the same time because Rumspringa showed her a whole new world, but that world did not include her family, and it did include James and Meg.

From the night that Elizabeth and James danced together, Elizabeth felt a spark in her heart that no Amish man had ever given her. She felt the feeling of being light on her feet, a feeling that could hardly be described with words. When he smiled at her nothing could keep a smile off her face. Since the evening that Elizabeth and James danced together, the two kept their feelings under lock and key regarding their unspoken attraction. Megan, however, saw that James was into Elizabeth and perhaps Elizabeth was interested in James too, so she broke-up with James even though she liked him. In some strange way, Megan gave them her blessing and saw their relationship all the way to the altar.

Even as Elizabeth uttered the words, "I do, she felt her heart break in two. Her life forever was divided. Her heart, well, was even more so divided. Her decision to wed James came with the decision to leave her family. Now, she found herself even more torn and heartbroken, because she was without James. She received the phone call when she was sitting at home sewing little booties for their baby on the way. James' boss, Marshall Hoover, called from the bar, where James worked as a bartender. Marshall started speaking slowly in a hushed tone. That was when Elizabeth knew that something was wrong. Elizabeth always knew Marshall, in the short time she had known him, to be a man who spoke his mind, and didn't hold back.

The conversation came back to Elizabeth in pieces. She still couldn't remember all of it. There had been an accident... James wasn't feeling very well when he came into work.... James looked pale... he was pouring drinks... and then he collapsed on the floor. A bar patron called 911, but by the time the ambulance arrived he was already gone. Elizabeth kept running the phone call through her head as if somehow it would change things or bring James back. James had suffered a fatal heart attack. They didn't know that James had a heart condition, but apparently, he did. He was too young to die. She was too young to be a widow. But she was. Elizabeth Brenneman was a widow.

Chapter 2: Not the Only Broken Heart

Elizabeth Brenneman was not the only one with a broken heart. More than one fellow yearned to marry Elizabeth Brenneman and was devastated when Elizabeth unexpectedly fell in love on Rumspringa. Elizabeth was the kind of girl you knew would be a loving, caring wife, and a sweet and tender mother. Any young Amish boy would dream of being Elizabeth's husband up until the point when Elizabeth left the community for James. Although the Amish community agreed that it was too bad that Elizabeth's husband had died so suddenly and at such a young age, there were not so many suitors that were still in interested in Elizabeth. Who would want to marry a young pregnant widow with a baby on the way?

Elizabeth did not feel the need to marry again, but she did feel the fear of raising her baby boy alone. Three weeks after James died, she found herself at Lancaster Women and Babies' Hospital. She was pushing, pushing, with only Megan by her side. Megan remained dedicated to Elizabeth, out of love and also of a sense of duty, because she allowed and even encouraged Elizabeth to date James. Little did she know she would be next to Elizabeth's side without James, as she birthed her child. After James Brenneman was born, Elizabeth found herself unable to care for her own child. She felt that giving her boy, his father's name would give him a sense of pride one day, but she also wanted to honor her Amish heritage and gave her boy her own last name.

The problem with giving birth and grieving a dead husband at the same time was that it was simply impossible. James looked like his father which made it harder and easier at the same time. James Junior had a round face, with olive skin and a small tuft of dark brown hair on the top of his head. He made everyone smile and laugh, and even though Elizabeth was eligible to receive financial support from the government she did not want to raise her boy in the English word without his father. She chose to leave her home for her husband, but without her husband, Elizabeth suffered. Whatever glow James put in her step was taken away by his death. There was only one true option, returning home, destined to remain a widow for the rest of her life.

She feared the reaction of her parents who were naturally crushed when she told them she fell in love and wanted to marry an Englishmen. When her husband died that night in the bar serving drinks she couldn't even think to tell her parents. Her father rejected her when she left and couldn't handle the thought of Elizabeth leaving the family, her home, their home, the community. It took Elizabeth over a month after his death to send a message to her parents through a friend that he passed away. She never heard a response from her parents and assumed that they did not want anything to do with her again. That was certainly more than fair considering what she had done. Sometimes she wondered if God was punishing her for marrying James? Wasn't God a good God? A fair God? A just God? A loving God? Surely the God that she learned about from her family and her community would not want her to be like this. To be broken hearted and alone. She would return. She would go back and then what? Only God knew.

Chapter 3: Strange English Ways

There was a community meeting to decide the fate of the young and no longer naïve Elizabeth and her newborn son, James. Her parents seemed to be unable to face her return as it would bring shame to their family, and her former friends and neighbors did not want to say anything against the Brenneman family for fear that they would lose even their respect. In a strange way, even though the Brennnemans did not want to respect the request of their daughter to return with her son, nobody wanted to speak in favor of Elizabeth, except one, Wayne Bender.

Wayne Bender was not an important man in the community, but he was a male voice, and in the Amish community, elders and men received the most respect. Wayne had a strong, solid, sounding voice that echoed through the hall. "Do we not preach forgiveness? Do we not believe in giving the homeless a home? Do we not believe in clothing the naked? Do we not believe in caring for the sick?" asked Wayne. The Beatitudes were what Wayne preached. "How could we call ourselves the children of God if we turn against one of our own in her time of need? Can we deny the needs of her newborn son?" roared Wayne through the town hall.

There were murmurs among the people until one by one the townspeople agreed with Wayne. How could they forsake Elizabeth?

Even though her own parents were not quick to forgive, for certain, she was in her hour of need, as was her son. With Wayne's words, the community softened and agreed that something could be done. Finally, one of the elderly women in the community, Mary, stood up and spoke on her behalf. "Elizabeth and her boy can live in my spare shed that I'm not using anymore. It's not really a fit living space, but I hate to see a girl on the street with a little one. I would need some help to make it a livable area, a bed for the girl, a crib for the little boy, and a proper toilet and sink. I suppose it could really use a new coat of paint and the windows are a little loose too. They make an awful rattling sound in the wind," she stated.

Slowly others chimed in. "Mary, if you have the space, I can help you with the labor," said Mary's son, Solomon. Wayne immediately agreed that he could help with renovations too. Slowly, but surely, the voices of those wanting to help Elizabeth were much greater than those who remained silent or in objection. "Actually, my husband knows plumbing, I bet he can connect a toilet outdoors," said another neighbor. So, it was decided that they would accept the return of Elizabeth and her son, despite the situation being extremely unusual, and the fact that typically those who chose to leave the Amish community were never permitted to return.

Meanwhile, Elizabeth sat with her son James in her and her former husband's apartment in shock. As tears rolled down her cheek she caressed her sweet son's face. Everything about James reminded her of her husband. How could it be possible that God allowed her to be in this position? If God was so loving then why did bad things happen to good people? She saw so much of her husband was in her young son including his pleasant demeanor. The one thing that Elizabeth had to be thankful for was her son's never-ending smiles and his ability to sleep through the night. She started attending a widow's support group in the city, but went only twice, after she realized that all the attendees were at least over the age of 60, and Elizabeth was barely

22. The moderator of the support group, a soft-spoken elderly woman, Josefine Reagan, caught Elizabeth on the way out the door the second and last time she attended the group.

"My dear, I know you are hurting, I wish there was something I could do for you, and I see that you are struggling. I know this group, well... we just aren't quite your age group, but you're welcome to go to Water Street Rescue Mission. There they help a lot of people in need. They have even depression support groups and single mother's groups. I hope I'm not offending you my dear, and of course you're still more than welcome to come here, but I think there you might find what you are looking for," said Josefine, as she handed Elizabeth a pamphlet with the address and phone number of the Water Street Rescue Mission on it.

"Thanks, I appreciate it really, said Elizabeth as tears rolled down her face. Despite trying to control her emotions she couldn't help but feel everything. Why did she have to feel everything? Everything. Everything was okay before Rumspringa. She began to feel an anger building up inside her, a feeling that she was not used to experiencing. Anger. It's just a stage of grief. That's what the therapist at the hospital had told her after James had passed away. The therapist, much like everyone else, handed her a card with her phone number on it and offered support, but whatever support the modern English word could offer could not compare with what support her home community would offer her if they accepted her back.

Elizabeth almost forgot that she was still standing in front of Josefine due to her scattered thoughts. She bid her goodbye and gave her an awkward half-hug before walking away. She did not turn around or even look at the woman's eyes. Josefine was doing the best she could, but Elizabeth knew already the support group was not going to be able to help her in any way. These women wanted to sit and sew and spew out good memories of all the years they spent with their husbands, of what their grown adult-age children were doing now, and how they enjoyed still being a part of the church, singing in the choir, cleaning the pews and dusting the statues.

While listening to the English widows speak, she longed for her own church community and a proper upbringing for her son. As she reached her apartment door she knew she was already resolved to return if they would have her back. She crumpled up the Water Street Rescue Mission pamphlet with her right hand and threw it on the ground as she turned the key to her apartment with her left hand. She wondered if her little boy would be left-handed like herself or right-handed like her father. Amidst her thoughts, she decided that even though her parents never returned her message but she would go, nonetheless.

Chapter 4: Healing Takes a Lifetime

Megan and Elizabeth sat together in the same diner where Elizabeth first met James, each drinking a coffee. Megan wanted Elizabeth to remember something special and at least their friendship. As a gesture of their friendship and where they came from, Megan asked Elizabeth to come out of her apartment and meet her one last time at the diner for "old time's sake." Elizabeth brought little James Junior in tow on her back. Elizabeth ordered her favorite breakfast for dinner, something that would typically never be allowed in her community. This was, after all, supposed to be a celebration of friendship. Not everything could be gray skies and tears forever.

Crispy hash browns, a Belgian waffle smothered a butter and sugary syrup, four slices of beef bacon, and a glass of apple juice. For certain this meal was a sin, but they were all of Elizabeth's favorite English breakfast foods. She had never seen so many carbohydrates that tasted so good yet so different from the flavors of home. She could not imagine her mother connecting electricity to the house, let alone using a waffle iron like the ones they used in the diner. For a few moments, Elizabeth found her laughing and smiling with Meg and baby James.

Meg asked Elizabeth, "Do you remember when I brought James to the diner, and you met him for the first time?" "How could I forget?" asked Elizabeth, somewhat happy and somewhat sad to be reminded of her dead husband. "You know girl, if you were anybody else, I would have called you a boyfriend stealer!" shouted Meg, a little louder than necessary. The waitress glared at Meg a little but none of the customers raised their heads even a little or dared to look at the two girls and the baby at the table by the window, creating more noise than usual. Their usual waitress was absent and she would never have said a thing, as she knew everything, well... almost everything about their lives. Regardless, Elizabeth attempted to shush Meg, which made the two only laugh louder. Not to mention that milk squirted through Meg's noise and went all over the table.

After an hour or so Elizabeth found herself reminded of her new responsibilities and her new life. "Meg, really, thank you so much, for everything, I mean it, but you know I have to go back," said Elizabeth. "I know," said Meg. "I love you, really, but James and I... we need a family. We are a family, but we have to go back. It's time for this little kiddo to meet his grandparents. I hope they want to meet us," stated Elizabeth. "You know girl, you got some courage!" said Meg. "Let's hit the road, shall we?" asked Elizabeth. "Damn, girl, you are practically an 'English lady' already. You and your non-Amish phrases like, 'let's hit the road.' I'm gonna miss you toots!" pronounced Meg.

As the two left the room, Elizabeth glanced around the diner, took mental snapshots in her mind of the room, her friendship with Meg, and even the food. She looked down at baby James, cooed him to sleep, and the two took off in the car for one last ride in the country together. Although they hoped it wouldn't be the last, they had to be a bit realistic. The wind wiped in circles around their bodies. Meg felt the time slipping away as the sun dipped below the horizon. Reds mixed with oranges colored the sky. Tall corn stalks dotted the countryside and the radio played Sia's "*No Cheap Thrills*," as they curved around Lancaster County's corners. For a moment, just a moment, Elizabeth laughed a true laugh.

Chapter 5: Whatever Shall Come, Will Come

Wayne stood in front of Mary's shed and considered all the work that would need to be done in order to make it livable for a young mother like Elizabeth. It certainly wasn't a palace, but it could be home with the help of the community. In the end, about 60% of the community had agreed to pitch in materials and labor to make the shed a home for Elizabeth and James Junior. Elizabeth's parents, however, remained silent on the matter, as they suffered from their own struggle of having felt rejected from their daughter when she chose to marry an Englishman. After all, who could blame them for having more than mixed feelings about their daughter's expected return? Although Elizabeth had not explicitly stated that she would return it was understood by her message to her parents that this was the best possible outcome for her and her newborn.

While Elizabeth struggled with the thought of raising James alone and the possible innumerable number of reactions her parents could have to her request to returning to the community, Wayne assembled a building crew. Wayne gathered some of the community's best painters, plumbers, wood workers, and gardeners. Fortunately for Elizabeth, it was the growing season and if seeds were planted now Elizabeth would at least have a wide array of fruits and vegetables ready for her to eat in the summer, and she could freeze anything she could not eat.

One of the best things about the Amish community was how they stood together in solidarity. As Elizabeth was packing her bags and negotiating the remaining payment on the lease with her landlord, Wayne and his assembled team added an extra small room to the shed. They knocked out a wall and created a bedroom for Elizabeth and her son. In the main "room" someone had donated a wood-burning stove and another community member donated an armchair. Quickly the additional room was added to the shed, which was to be Elizabeth's new home. Behind the shed, a few of the woman worked the land, turned the soil, and planted seeds so that Elizabeth could have an abundance of food in a few months. A plumber installed an outdoor toilet in an adjacent building, and within the day the space looked like someone could actually like there. It was no longer just a place for sheep, ox, and or even a working man's tools. It was a home.

Wayne, however, had another interest in helping Elizabeth, besides his altruistic reason. Since he was no more than 15 he had his eyes on Elizabeth. Never, never, in a thousand years could he have imagined that Elizabeth would fall in love with an Englishman while on Rumspringa, nor, could he believe that perhaps he was getting his second chance to be with Elizabeth. He desired so much to be with her and also to be a father. Someone needed to be a father to the little boy, and even if she would not have her, James needed a man in his life to teach him about life and to show him the ways of the world, not just the Amish world, but also even the English world. He should be able to make his own decision one day about whether or not he wanted to return to the English world of his father or stay Amish. Undoubtedly, Elizabeth would want her son to be baptized in the church when she returned.

Wayne was counting on her returning. How would he explain to the community that they had prepared a place for her and her newborn to live if she never came back? Wayne resolved that, as per Amish custom, all things had to be determined with a calm mind and a steady fist. Since he had neither of those at the moment, he made his way to his father's house to see if he was okay. Ever since his mother died, his father struggled to feel himself. Even though he always appeared to be himself to the public, he knew that on the inside he struggled.

The night air was thin, the stars shined more brightly than the previous nights as there was not a cloud in sight. He remembered a multitude of nights from when he was a boy that he longed to view the stars, but the sky remained covered in clouds and blocked his beautiful view. The city of Lancaster, albeit, not a very large one, compared to other English cities, still also created light pollution that sometimes also affected his ability to see the stars. Tonight, however, was simply perfect. The stars were aligned in the sky and brightly lit as if the stars knew his deepest desires.

Chapter 6: The Birth of a New Day

Aside from a few sentimental items and several English gadgets that Elizabeth decided to keep, she more or less abandoned her English life. Her husband's watch and wedding ring, several English novels, fine china that was a wedding gift from Meg, wedding photos, English drink mix called Kool-Aid, and a roll of duct tape all made her suitcases but what Elizabeth could not carry in her suitcase she left to Meg. A return to her roots, to simplicity, was what she and James needed now if they were going to be okay.

As Elizabeth approached the home of her Aunt Abigail with baby James and her few belongings she felt herself shake inside with fear. She knocked lightly on the door and was relieved when her Aunt Abigail was overjoyed to see her return. "Oh, my dear, Elizabeth. I'm so sorry, I could not believe when I heard the news. This must be James Junior. What a sweet little boy you have, Liz," pronounced Elizabeth's aunt. "Oh well, I guess I can't just leave you standing on the doorstep like this, do come in," said Aunt Abigail.

"Um, Aunt Abigail, have you heard from my parents? Will they accept my return?" asked Elizabeth as she crossed the threshold of her Aunt's home. "Oh, don't worry about them, they'll come around. We're happy to have you home again. Don't listen to everything everyone says around here, you know how they are. Not everyone here agrees about anything, ever. You're not exactly new to these parts," said Aunt Abigail.

"Sorry to ask, but do you think there is a room I can nurse James?" asked Elizabeth. "It is his feeding time, and I don't want to make him wait too much longer." Elizabeth's Auntie led her down the hallway to her own bedroom, paused, opened the door just a crack, and said to her, "You know, I'm sorry we don't have enough space for you here but the community did do something for you that I think you'll like. You know who started the whole thing? That Wayne boy...he's a good boy, Elizabeth. You ought to thank him when you see him." "Oh, really," stated Elizabeth in a surprised manner. "I can't return to my parents' house?

she inquired. Not right now, Darlin', but don't you worry, everything will be okay."

After Elizabeth nursed James, Aunt Abigail recommended that they go and speak with Wayne and the owner of the small home where Elizabeth could stay. Her Aunt Abigail explained in a long-winded fashion the entire story about how nobody wanted to step up and help except Wayne, but one by one he had gained support from the majority of the community. When they arrived at the former shed which was now transformed into a miniature home, Elizabeth sighed relief and met the owner of the home. Thanking her profusely, she started to cry, thinking about where she came from and the road she had yet to cross. With tears of gratitude, she placed her bags down inside the home and gently placed James in a new crib which someone had built for her. Her tears were mixed with joy and sadness, but at least, she was home again.

The next day, Wayne came by the house to see if Elizabeth was settling into her home with James. "Good afternoon Miss Elizabeth, I see that you've made yourself at home. I just wanted to make sure you were alright since you're here alone with this cute little guy," said Wayne as he smiled at both Elizabeth and baby James. "Yes, thank you so much for everything you've done. Really, I could never have imagined that someone could do all of this for me, well, for us," replied Elizabeth. "Truly, you are an angel from heaven," continued Elizabeth.

"No, please, I'm just helping where I can," answered Wayne. "I can come back tomorrow and see if you're doing okay," he offered. "It's not necessary at all, but thank you very much," affirmed Elizabeth. "Can I get you anything to drink Wayne?" she asked. "If it's not too much trouble I would drink a glass of water," replied Wayne. "No trouble at all, really," said Elizabeth as she poured two glasses of water, one for each of them.

"So, how are you doing, Wayne? I haven't heard from you, of course, since before I left the community? Are you still helping with your family's farm? How is your mother? I always thought she was a lovely lady," acknowledged Elizabeth. "Thank you for asking, but I'm sorry to say that my mother passed away. She was always very ill when I was growing up," said Wayne. "Oh, I'm so terribly sorry. I didn't know. I feel awful," cried Elizabeth. "How could you have known? It's hard for me, but more so for my father. He's loved her since they were kids," acknowledged Wayne. "Now that it's just my father and me at the house there is also a lot of work to go around, but we manage alright," said Wayne. "I wish there was something I could do for you after all you have done for me," echoed Elizabeth.

"Just take care of yourself and your baby. I promise that I will come by the house when I can, even if you tell me not to. Only if you insist that I am not welcome, I will not come," said Wayne. "Well then, I guess, James and I wouldn't mind some company once in a while," she replied. "I apologize Ms. Elizabeth, but I have to meet my father for dinner. You won't mind if I leave, will you?" asked Wayne. "No, not at all," whispered Elizabeth, despite the fact that she was enjoying the company and a distraction from her heartache.

As Wayne excused himself and sauntered towards the door, Elizabeth followed him to the door to see him out, and Wayne extended his hand for a handshake, but Elizabeth decided a hug would be much more appropriate given the circumstance. Wayne's arms enclosed around Elizabeth like the wings of a dove, and she felt her spirit lifted by his warmth, his presence, and his support. Elizabeth found herself hugging him with an intensity that she did not expect, but she relished the embrace even after he had departed from her home. She found herself thinking about the hug from Wayne, but to the same extent she couldn't help but remember the feel of hugs from her husband. She was upset that she was starting to forget his smell. She had saved one of his favorite t-shirts, but his smell had long since disappeared from the shirt. Whilst the night folded around Elizabeth, baby James fell fast asleep in his new crib, and Elizabeth's eyed drooped and shut.

Chapter 7: From a Widow's Window

Despite Elizabeth's insistence that Wayne did not need to stop by the house on a daily basis, Wayne was true to his word, as a captain is to his crew during a storm at sea. Elizabeth had her own storm at sea, so to speak, and Wayne had slowly become her anchor. Elizabeth had never thought of Wayne in any other way than platonic before, but his frequent visits to the house gave her hope that James would have a semi-normal childhood. As she washed the dishes she caught herself looking out the window and watching Wayne hold little James. Her heart broke as she saw how good Wayne was with her baby, but she winced when she thought about how it should have been her husband holding James. She turned away quickly as she did not want the others to think additional bad things about her. As it was, the entire community seemed to be on edge with her decision to return to the community. Such a situation was completely unheard of, until her actually.

Even after turning away from the window she glanced again out the window at Wayne and James. Wayne reminded her oddly of her deceased husband, but only in a few ways. Elizabeth imagined that if her husband had been the chance to be a father to their baby he would have held little James the same way. Elizabeth couldn't seem to keep up with caring for James, herself, and the home, but Wayne was quite faithful in helping her. It seemed almost too nice. Who comes almost every day to care for a young widow, unless... thought Elizabeth... unless

Wayne had other interests. It finally occurred to her that Wayne maybe was interested in Elizabeth despite being a widow with a baby. Wayne saw her looking out the window at him. She waved innocently and quickly diverted her eyes back to her dishes, so she could pretend that she wasn't looking intentionally.

The problem was that Elizabeth felt torn emotionally in so many ways that she didn't know if she could be with someone else again ever. She didn't know if she should feel guilty for maybe even considering that she *MIGHT* like Wayne and that Wayne *MIGHT* like her. She felt *almost* like she did when she noticed that she had feelings for James after the first time they met. As guilt sunk in her smile turned upside down. Wayne re-entered the cottage shortly thereafter with baby James asleep in his arms. Although he could see something was wrong he didn't dare to ask what it was. He realized that they both were staring at each other through the window, but that probably was not a good topic of conversation.

"Well, can I help you with anything else? You sure look tired? I could watch James while you get some rest. He's asleep anyway. It's really no trouble at all Liz... Elizabeth. Sorry," stated Wayne. "You can call me Liz, it's not a problem. You don't have to be embarrassed. It's just, I'm amazed that you come here every day to help us. I'm certain that you have other people to care for, like yourself too, sometimes. Don't you think?" commented Elizabeth.

"Of course, but a good Amish man always respects an upstanding lady like yourself," replied Wayne. "If I didn't know any better, I'd think you were trying to charm me," said Elizabeth as she laughed and felt herself blush a little. "Well, maybe I am," Wayne said as he laughed a little before he continued, "I better be going then. I have to water the field. It's been hot these days and the crops just aren't growing like they should be." "Sure, good night then, and thank you, really," said Elizabeth. "Good night Liz," echoed Wayne as he walked away while a smile grew across his face.

Chapter 8: Baby Steps

The days passed for Wayne is a similar fashion. He worked the fields in the very early morning with his father. He prepared a light lunch for him and his father, took an afternoon siesta and then went to Liz's house around 3 pm every day, like clockwork. Wayne enjoyed his daily pattern but longed for something more with Liz. Although he didn't want to push her, especially considering that the two-year anniversary of her husband's death was approaching, he felt pulled towards her. Two years was more than one, but he knew very well that the heart healed only with time. Much as he felt with the passing of his own mother, he learned by day to grieve, but also to love, laugh, and smile again. Perhaps an even larger blessing than Liz or his father in his life was little baby James. Little baby James was not so little anymore and was growing into a healthy boy.

The first day that James took his first steps Wayne was at the house to watch him walk. While James walked to his mother, Elizabeth, who caught him and held him delicately in his arms, Wayne could not resist his own tears. Almost everything he could have dreamed of happening was already coming true. He didn't need to know everything, he didn't need to know the future with Liz and her son because in that moment everything was okay. In the face of everything they had passed together and separately, Elizabeth was coming to understand that everything he had done for her was not just out of respect, but also because he cared for her deeply.

Baby James turned with the help of his mother and started to take a few steps towards Wayne and uttered one syllable. Da. Wayne and Elizabeth could not have been happier or sadder as James grew and as they witnessed James walk and speak the word Da. In any case, Wayne was not James' biological father, but he was his father now, as much as his Elizabeth's husband was, if not more.

A few things were still missing from Elizabeth's life, including the acceptance of her parents and an understanding of what her relationship with Wayne was, but she stopped questioning it and accepted life as it was. She thought less about the English world, but she did occasionally receive visits from Meg, who wholeheartedly approved of Wayne, but did not yet utter it out loud. At least, in these moments, Elizabeth found peace, and her sense of self once more. She had an identity not just as a widow, but more importantly as a mother, a woman, and a friend. There were times, of course, that she still wondered what her life would be like if her husband had not passed away suddenly and unexpectedly, but she recognized that God was with her and would protect her always, and in a way, Wayne was the Holy Spirit, her dove, and little James, her son, symbolized Jesus Christ.

The stars were not always aligned in her favor, but a certain coffee-stained mug on her kitchen table was never empty to her. It was imperfect, but it was perfect to her. It was chipped on one side and the imperfectness of the mug was apparent to any stranger in her home, but to Elizabeth, the mug was like her home. The red lines across the center of the mug were slightly faded from use, and in her mind, the missing piece simply added character. Recently, a bright blue thumbprint had been added to the mug since James took a liking to paint. In spite of everything, life was whole, as whole as it could be, if you were a young Amish widow.

THE LOVE LIFE OF BRIDGET PERRY

VIOLET BOONE

Bridget Perry flipped down the visor against the afternoon sun as she steered in sweeping curves along the coastal road. She drew in her breath sharply. Her wrists hurt. She glanced at her wrists which were bruised and swollen and then averted her eyes. She didn't want to be reminded of them or of the event that caused them.

For the umpteenth time that day, tears welled in her eyes and spilled down her cheeks. Not even the stunning beauty of an Australian sunset could distract her from the heaviness in her heart. Images of her ex, came unbidden to her mind; his fathomless black eyes and raven hair falling long and wavy down his muscled back; his teeth white against swarthy skin. Bridget's breath caught in her throat. "Jackson," she whispered through her tears. She sighed one long shuddering miserable breath. Why was she crying over that two-timing, heartless pig anyway? Because I don't know how to be by myself, was the honest answer.

Bridget squinted and slowed down. With the sun at this angle she could barely see a few feet in front of her. She rounded the bend at a crawl and noticed a small motel sitting back away from the road, shrouded in thick foliage; a wooden sign peeped out from behind a heavy overhang of magenta flowers; Bougainvillea lodge it said in a cursive blue letters. Suddenly, Bridget wanted nothing more than to stop at here away from the sun, where she would be able to rest and recuperate. She pulled in and the gravel crunched in welcome as she parked the car. She stifled a groan. Sitting in the car for fourteen hours straight had done its work on her muscles. As she pulled herself out of the car and stretched her arms behind her head, she caught a glimpse of the view. Bougainvillea lodge had a perfect position facing the beach, which was, to her great relief, devoid of crowds, except for a lone walker and his dog and a young couple with small children paddling in the shallows.

The woman behind the counter welcomed her with just the right balance of warmth and respect for privacy that she needed, giving her a key and reminding her that dinner would be served at the restaurant at six. With slow deliberate steps, Bridget carried her bag, packed in such haste the night before and now she realized depressingly light, to her room. Not doubting that she had left most of her best clothes and belongings behind, she looked around the room. Nothing special, she thought, but adequate for her needs. The bathroom looked clean enough and turning back the bed, she was pleased to find crisp white cotton sheets. Right now that was all the mattered, a hot shower and sleep.

With her clothes strewn across the bathroom floor, she winced with pleasure as the hot water pummelled her tired and sore shoulders. She lathered up every part of her body and scrubbed. What she was scrubbing away she wasn't sure, but the need to be clean was overwhelming. There was more crying, but this time, the tears were more from relief than sadness. It felt good to be alone where no one could reach her or find her. She was so tired. It was all she could do to dry herself off and pull on some clean underwear and a t-shirt and crawl, exhausted into bed.

When she opened her eyes the room was dark with one brilliant shard of light spilling through a gap in the heavy drapes. Bridget reached out and felt her way over the bedside table for her phone. Her home screen glowed with a photo of Jackson during their holiday to Bali the year before. She frowned at it and focused on the time instead – 11.am! She flopped back on the pillows for a minute, amazed at how long she had slept. She lay there listening to her body. She felt relaxed and for the first time in ten months, safe.

Last April, Jackson had walked into her life and turned it upside down. He was mesmerizing in his masculine beauty. She was the envy of women wherever they went; she saw it in their eyes. Women, who ordinarily were shy and mousey, became predatory and catlike in his presence. He was talented, funny, and charming in public; but it hadn't taken long for her to realize that behind closed doors he was a cold, narcissistic bully. Ten months of verbal put-downs had left her believing that no other man would ever tolerate her the way he did. She had suspected cheating but had never been able to find any definitive evidence. He didn't need to cheat behind her back anyway. He was happy enough to flirt with other women right under her nose. On the rare occasion she called him out on it, he would jeer and tell her she was lucky to be with him and to leave if she didn't like it.

She didn't like it, but she didn't dare leave. Her best friend Nick had voiced his disapproval over and over. The image of him clenching his large, usually gentle, hands in frustration, came to mind. Dear, loyal Nick, with his lanky frame, round blue eyes, and freckled upturned nose, exactly the same as it had been when they played together as five-year-olds. He had always been there and she couldn't imagine the world without him in it. Some people winked and hinted that they would one day end up together, but she had always laughed at the idea. Nick was so safe. She knew him possibly better than she knew herself sometimes and she wanted mystery and adventure. As a result, her attention was too readily arrested by men who were exciting and unavailable in some way.

"It ticks me off," Nick had grumbled one day a few weeks into her relationship with Jackson. They were sitting on her couch watching re-runs of Seinfeld and eating chips.

"What ticks you off?"

"You, and other women too, always gushing slavishly over wankers like Jackass, I mean Jackson." He smiled wickedly. "What is it with women and bad boys? Do you actually want to be treated like crap?"

Bridget threw a cushion at Nick's head messing up the top of his straight brown hair. "He's not that bad!" She dodged the cushion on its return flight. "I don't know why but there's just something irresistible about a man who might not hang around. Knowing that he might go, but he's choosing to stay with me is sort of exciting, y'know?"

Nick's expression was incredulous. "No, I don't know! Bridge' that's the most ludicrous idea. The guy doesn't care about you! He puts you down! People don't do that to people they love, can't you see that?"

"He's had a rough life!" she countered. "His dad was a deadbeat. His mom had different men parading through his childhood. He didn't get shown much love and I want to make up for that. I think I can heal him if I love him enough."

Nick had stared at her long and hard, finally pulling her to him in a warm hug. "That isn't love Bridget. That's not how love works. Love isn't a one-way thing. It's like water." He pulled back and looked Bridget in the face. "Love is like water and people are like sponges. If you pour love into someone they should soak it up like a sponge, but if a person is like a rock, then the love just splashes and runs off the side getting wasted on the ground. Jackson's heart is a rock. You're wasting your love on him."

He had gone home after that and Bridget had thought about his analogy many times since then. It had all come to a head when last night after work, she had gone into their bathroom and found a woman's earring in the sink. She had confronted Jackson about it when he got home drunk in the early hours of the next morning, and instead of lying or being ashamed, he had mocked her and told her that the earring woman was here to stay and she could take it or leave it. She had screamed and thrown herself at him in a panicked rage and that was when he had grabbed her by the wrists twisting them cruelly and making her sink to the floor, a defeated wreck. She had packed a hurried bag and left there and then, not thinking or looking back and now 30 hours later she was here, alone, and finally free.

Pulling back the drapes of her motel room revealed a glorious Summer's day. From her window, the water glistened and the sand glowed white in the sun. It was much busier today. What had seemed like an empty country road the night before was now fringed with parked cars baking in the heat. Families strolled up and down and from the beach; the sounds of laughter and excited yelps carried across to her window.

Bridget threw on a pair of lavender shorts and a white cheesecloth peasant blouse. She looked at herself critically in the mirror. Her eyes still had a residue of puffiness from all the crying and over-sleeping but she didn't feel like wearing make-up. Her face stared back at her in solemn comradery. At 27, Bridget could still boast clear, olive skin with a smattering of freckles. Her best features apparently, were her large hazel eyes and long auburn hair. She curled her lip; obviously, Jackson didn't think they were that great. Before she could let her thoughts wander gloomily down that road, she pulled herself away from the mirror, grabbed her bag and left the room.

The air was balmy on her skin and the sound of her sandals slapping against the cool tiles brought a delicious sensation of Summer holidays bubbling up inside her. It seemed like the real Bridget was struggling up in revolt against the old, Jackson oppressed, Bridget, desperate to make a comeback. The lady behind the desk welcomed her with a smile.

"Nice day for it," she beamed. "Heading down to the beach?"

"Yep, just going for a stroll. It's busier than I expected it to be."

"That's because the agricultural show is on in Bluegum this week. When people get too hot traipsing around the showgrounds they inevitably end up here at Opal Bay to cool off. Are you going to the show today?"

Bridget let her mind wander for a moment. She imagined the showgrounds packed with hot sweaty people, crying children, loud music, and smelly livestock. She shook her head, smiling. "No, I think I'll just enjoy a peaceful day on the beach, thanks. How much are those straw hats?"

"That'll put you back ten dollars, love."

Bridget chose a broad-brimmed straw hat with a yellow and white polka-dot band. As she closed the door of the reception office behind her, she was hit with a wall of heat. In the scramble of departure, she hadn't thought to pack things like sunscreen. Without it, she was going to end the day red as a lobster, but throwing caution to the wind, she stepped out into the day with a 'come what may' attitude. She followed the sounds of laughter, seagulls, and surf across the road and through a scrubby pathway cut through the sand, slowing down against the resistance of the sand, panting a little at the effort. A couple of pre-teen boys hurtled past her, laughing like hyenas. They missed her by inches, covering her with sand in the process. She laughed out loud. She couldn't be angry. Their innocence was unapologetically refreshing.

An enticing aroma wafted over to her from a food stand that had been set up on the beach under a canopy. It was a sausage sizzle. Bridget's stomach growled; she hadn't given food a second thought since leaving Jackson, and now, all of a sudden, she felt that she could devour an entire side of beef. Two long lines of hungry beachgoers had formed at the stand, so Bridget took her place behind an elderly woman baked brown and wrinkled from a lifetime spent on Aussie beaches. Everyone was buying as much as they could in one go, and the line was moving slowly, so Bridget found herself watching the other people in the queue.

In the line next to her and a few places ahead, a tall person caught her eye. Bleached blond hair over a pair of broad tanned shoulders, tapering down to slim hips in turquoise board shorts made her smile in appreciation. She hoped he would turn around so that she could see his face. Come on, she urged mentally, turn around just a little bit. As if he heard her thoughts, the tall man turned and looked straight at her with startling blue eyes. He held her gaze just for a second and then turned back. Bridget felt like she had been hit by a sledgehammer. A very gorgeous, beach-babe kind of sledgehammer. "Just like Captain America," she murmured inwardly.

"You're too right about that, love."

Startled, Bridget looked down to see the old lady beaming up at her. "Did I say that out aloud?" she gasped, mortified.

"Yeah, but who could blame you?" The old lady looked dreamily over at the handsome man and sighed. "If I was fifty years younger, he'd be in trouble, that's all I can say."

Bridget giggled and chatted with the old lady until at last, she got to the top of the line and bought her food which she ate at the base of some dunes further up the beach. Every now and then she would search the water to locate the tall blond. He was easy to spot in his turquoise board shorts out in the surf catching a few waves. It was nice to watch him unobserved from her vantage point. Occasionally, she would acknowledge a twinge of guilt over looking at a man other than Jackson, and then the truth would come slamming down like a judge's gavel. Verdict - Jackson isn't yours, Bridget. He never was. He doesn't love you. It's over. Then the real Bridget would push again from within. The indignant Bridget, the proud Bridget, encouraging and boosting her confidence a smidgen further. It was a sensation she welcomed back with open arms.

From her spot on the beach, the sapphire-blue water looked so tempting, she regretted not bringing something to swim in. But there was no reason not to get at least a little bit wet. She unfolded her stiff muscles and made her way down to the water's edge, wading in till the water came up to her knees. Keeping to the shallows, Bridget splashed along, stopping here and there to pick up a pretty shell which she tucked into the pocket of her shorts. An urgent shout somewhere behind her, made Bridget turn around. Further back where she had been sitting, a woman was screaming for help. Some people were stopping and looking at her with concern. Although Bridget couldn't hear, she could see they were asking her what was the matter. Others, Bridget noticed in angry amazement, had pulled their phones out and were recording the scene. And then Bridget saw it, at the woman's feet, a small limp body lay in the sand. Without a second thought, Bridget started to run. Where were the lifeguards? She'd seen their watch tower about five hundred meters up the beach. As she ran, she shouted at anyone who would listen. "Call the lifeguards! Unconscious child on the beach!" Bridget fell momentarily and was up in an instant, sprinting as hard as her legs would carry her. Out of the corner of her eye, another figure was running up from the water. It was Turquoise board shorts, hurtling along like some kind of superhero toward the screaming woman. Bridget arrived panting heavily at the woman's side. What she saw made her heart sink.

"My boy! Help my boy! A Bluebottle stung him. I think he's allergic!"

Without answering, Bridget sank to her knees by the little boy. He looked about five and his lips were blue. Across his torso and upper arms were the tell-tale red welts of a jellyfish sting. Bluebottles were painful but not usually dangerous. If this child was experiencing anaphylactic shock, he could die. She shouted again for someone to get the lifeguards and then, summoning everything she had learned in First Aid at school, she immediately began CPR. Beside her, the boy's mother was kneeling over them now with silent tears coursing down her face. Bridget was also aware of Turquoise board shorts beside her assessing the situation.

"What's going on? Are you trained?" he was asking Bridget. She shook her head.

"Bluebottle sting. Possible allergic reaction."

"Then let me help; you breathe; I'll do the compressions."

Together, the two of them continued to work on the little boy with the hushed, expectant crowd watching on. Bridget wondered if they were making any difference at all when finally, after what seemed an age, the crowd parted for two lifeguards, who quickly assessed the situation, and took over. Relieved, Bridget and Turquoise board shorts, moved away, shaking and exhausted from the adrenaline coursing through their veins. They stood leaning on each other watching on as the lifeguards worked. Bridget found herself praying repeatedly; please God, don't let him die? The silence around them was heavy, broken only by the sounds of the lifeguards working on the little boy and the mournful call of gulls. The waves rolled into shore rhythmically as though they were trying to drum life back into the child.

A sudden noise split the quiet. A wet splutter and a weak cough, and then thank heaven, a louder choke and cough, and then a cry! An unearthly wail burst from the little boy's mother as she realized her son wasn't dead and a cheer rose from the crowd. Bridget found herself turning to congratulate Turquoise board shorts only to find that he had left. When did that happen? She scanned the beach without success. He was nowhere to be seen. Bridget turned back to watch the little boy being carried off on a stretcher. His mother paused a moment to hug her and thank her.

"Thank you so much, I think you saved my little boy's life! Please thank your boyfriend for me okay?" She hurried off to follow her son and the crowd dispersed. Bridget stood there, suddenly deflated after the intensity of the experience. For some reason, the beach had lost its attraction and her thoughts turned to the Agricultural show. Maybe it wouldn't be such a bad idea to go for an hour or two?

Half an hour later she was entering the town of Bluegum having first gone back to the motel for a change of clothes. It was easy to find the showgrounds. Street signs directing the traffic to the show were on every corner. Pedestrians seemed to have only one destination, and when she pulled into carpark she could see that there was still a bit of a queue to buy tickets. Bridget entered the grounds through an old-fashioned turnstile joining the throng of hot and tired patrons trying to navigate the crowds. The festival was in full swing with Ferris wheels and Dodgem cars, side shows, and fairy floss stands. She passed huge barns and stables which housed all of the prize winning livestock. The smell of manure wafted out making Bridget's nostrils twitch. Ugh, she thought, immediately regretting her decision. What she needed was somewhere she could just sit and be entertained for a while. Reflecting on childhood visits to the Royal Melbourne Show, a particularly fond memory popped into her head. The Grand Arena, of course! She would go and watch the parades of animals, the horse tricks, the clowns and daredevil acts and maybe even wait till evening for the firework display.

Bridget decided to just follow the general flow of pedestrians, stopping here and there to look at displays on the way. On the corner of an intersection was an old fashioned American style diner where they sold snacks and takeaway food. As she passed she could see into the diner. People were sitting, chatting and eating in the leather upholstered booths. She was hungry, but she wasn't in the mood for hotdogs. She was just about to cross the road and stop at a place selling kebabs when out of the corner of her eye she glimpsed a flash of blond hair. Bridget stopped dead in her tracks causing a man and woman to crash into her from behind.

"Watch where you're bloody going!"

Bridget wasn't sure if she apologized or not. She actually didn't care, because there, shoving a hot dog into his beautiful mouth, was Turquoise board shorts, in the American Diner! Before embarrassment, fear, or good judgment could stop her, she had climbed the few steps and walked through the glass doors. He didn't look up; he was too engrossed in his meal to notice. Bridget found herself standing by his booth with a shy grin on her face.

"Hi."

Turquoise board shorts started. His wide blue eyes opening even wider at the sight of her. "Hey!" He struggled to stand up but got hooked up on the corner of the table, jabbing his hip and making him wince. He smiled through the pain, extending his hand to her. "Hey, it's you, the CPR girl!"

"Yep, it's me. I was just passing and happened to see you. You left so quickly at the beach, I was hoping to introduce myself and thank you for your help... do you mind if I join you?"

"No, not at all, no worries, I'd enjoy you... I mean, that would be nice."

Bridget slid into the booth across from him and they appraised each other for a couple of seconds.

"I'm Bridget, and you are?"

"Daniel, Daniel Inglis."

"You say that like you're James Bond or something." Bridget ran her hand through her hair and twiddled with a loose curl at the end. "Actually, you did look a bit like James Bond running up the beach like that to save the day."

Daniel grimaced. "Oh, no, did I? How embarrassing. Well, you were doing a bit of a Wonder woman yourself. It was quite impressive."

Bridget laughed. "We should have our own show!" They were interrupted by a waitress who took Bridget's order. Bridget continued, "So, do you live locally?"

"No." Just on a trip for work and passing through. You?"

Bridget sighed, wondering how much she should say. "No, I'm not local. I guess you could say I'm a city girl looking to make a sea change. I'm on the hunt for a new place to establish some roots and start a new life." She stopped wondering if she had said too much. Daniel seemed to understand and didn't pry any further.

"That sounds quite an appealing idea actually. I think we all could benefit from starting afresh once in a while. What do you do for a crust?"

"I'm a teacher, and I run an online business writing résumés and cover letters." She narrowed her eyes at him, thinking. "Hmm, let me see if I can guess what you are. You look like you could be a doctor... am I close?"

"Well, I am in the business of taking care of people so you're right there. I guess you could say I'm a social worker of sorts."

Bridget absorbed the information in happy disbelief; this guy was almost too good to be true. A social worker meant he was someone who cared about people, not only that, he was polite, unpretentious, and of course drop dead gorgeous. And the best thing about him, she decided, was that he was the absolute opposite of Jackson. All of the feelings of longing and hurt about Jackson dissolved right there in that diner booth. It fizzled into nothing so quickly she was shocked into stark realization of what she had been succumbing herself to for the past ten months. The understanding that not only had Jackson never loved her but that she had never loved him was as plain as the nose on her face. Across from her Daniel was looking at her with one eyebrow raised and a crooked smile.

"By the look on your face, my job description doesn't meet with your approval."

"What? Oh, no! I think it's a wonderful, honorable kind of work... No, if I looked odd, I was thinking of how different you are to someone I know."

Daniel was quiet, focusing his attention on removing the cherry from the top of his Ice-cream Sundae. It slipped off the edge of his spoon and slid down the side of his glass onto the plate; his eyes traveled from his plate to the bruises on her wrists. "Is that someone you're running away from?" His blue eyes looked up and held her in a questioning gaze for a moment before licking the ice-cream off his spoon. Bridget pulled her hands back under the table, her voice was mildly indignant.

"You could say that. But not running. Yesterday I was dragging myself away, but today I can say it's over. I've left and I'm never going back."

"Good."

Bridget looked up at him. He was looking at her steadily, knowingly. She took a deep breath. "And now I'm all alone like Nellie No Friends at the Bluegum Agricultural Show. I don't suppose I could twist your arm to spend the day with me? I'd feel silly going on the roller coaster by myself."

Daniel hesitated, but only for an instant. "Consider it twisted," he said with a grin.

They spent the rest of the afternoon having more fun than Bridget had experienced in what seemed like years. Daniel was funny and intelligent and insightful with an air of confidence that was deeply appealing. Never once did he utter a sexist remark or blurt obscenities or look her over like a piece of steak, like Jackson would have. In contrast, he was the consummate gentleman, helping her onto rides, walking ahead of her in the crowds to shield her from being jostled, and opening doors for her. Once or twice when standing in a queue she would feel his hand brush against hers or his hand on her arm protectively.

After the sun went down, they took their dinner to the Grand Arena to watch the fireworks. As they stood staring mesmerized like little children at the display, Bridget felt Daniel's arms slip around her waist from behind. She leaned into him, enjoying the hard warmth of his chest against her back and his mouth near her ear. Like this, it was difficult to concentrate on the fireworks because there were fireworks of another sort going off inside her. But, fighting to the surface of her consciousness, a small voice came unsolicited from the deepest recesses of her mind. It was a voice of – what was it a voice of, caution perhaps, or was it good judgment? Don't rush it was telling her, but the voice quickly became garbled and indistinct as she pushed it back where it came from.

Their conversation became slower and quieter after that. A different kind of language had taken over. Words were replaced by holding hands and shy caresses. As they walked back to Daniel's car the air was electric with the question – what next? There was a choice to be made. Was Daniel making the same choice? What was he thinking? She looked at him sideways out of the corner of her eye, as he fumbled with the car keys. He's nervous too, she realized. The trip home in the car was silent except for snippets of polite small talk. Neither of them wanted to destroy the mood, they were heading toward one conclusion for the night and they both knew it.

Daniel walked Bridget to her door; the light above had blown and they were standing, conveniently, in the shadows, away from prying eyes. She wondered if there was any point going through the usual end of date etiquette of thanking Daniel for a nice time, the invitation for a nightcap etc. He was still behind her, so she turned to face him and lifted her face to his. What she saw on his face startled her somewhat. His eyes that had been bright and blue all day, were now almost black; his pupils dilated to their fullest. There was an intensity there that both frightened her and bound her, unable to look away. She ran her tongue over her lips in anticipation and his eyes dropped to her mouth. When he spoke, his voice was hoarse.

"You have the most beautiful mouth."

Bridget's lips curled into a softly parted smile and she leaned in closer. He was going to kiss her. She closed her eyes and waited, focusing all of her attention on her mouth in anticipation. The night breeze on her moist lips was cool, and then his lips were there, warm, firm and full on hers. His arms went around her and lifted her up so that her toes were barely touching the ground. He held her so effortlessly that she let herself relax into the kiss. This was more like it; so much nicer than Jackson's hurried, rough embraces. A new idea came to her mind, wouldn't it be nice to leave it here and to let it remain sweet and romantic, to softly say goodnight and close the door in anticipation of another date? But as Daniel's kisses became more urgent, her resolve began to weaken. Self-control had never been her forte. She broke the kiss and pulled away. "Stay with me?" she whispered. Daniel nodded and followed her into the dark motel room and closed the door behind him with a click.

She was in a strange house with a corridor flanked by walls with garish lime wallpaper. The color made her nauseous. Along the walls were dozens of doors leading to dark rooms, which she entered panicked and fevered, looking for something, but she didn't know what. "I'm running out of time, running out of time!" The words ran in a loop over and over in her head, but the further she ran down the corridor the smaller it got and every room became more cramped, stifling her and filling her with desperate dread, until finally she was wedged tight and suffocating at the pointed end of the corridor, curled up in a ball.

Bridget woke with a start sitting bolt upright in the dawn light, covered in perspiration and her chest heaving. The dream, which was a reoccurring one, was still fresh in her mind, but she knew if she waited a minute it would fade. Then she remembered Daniel. Jerking her head around, she stared at the other side of the bed. It was rumpled, but empty. She scanned the room. He was gone. He had left nothing behind. A small white object on the sheet beside her caught her eye. It was the butt of a ticket for the roller coaster ride from the day before. Bridget lay back on the pillow staring with unseeing eyes at the tiny shred of paper. Last night had not been what she had expected. She had expected to wake up full and replete with Prince Charming breathing softly beside her. Instead, the experience had been furtive and intense. Daniel's set jaw and black eyes swam before her. There had been nothing magical about last night as she had hoped. A ball of regret began to form in the pit of her stomach. It was too soon after Jackson. She had known that last night. Why couldn't she just say no to men? Nick was going to have something to say about this when she told him.

The thought of unburdening herself to Nick gave her some comfort. The red digits on the bedside clock glowed 6:23; a bit early but he'd be getting up to get ready for work soon anyway. His phone rang out. She was hesitating, wondering whether she should try again when her phone began to vibrate; Nick's photo coming up on her screen. She swiped the screen with relief.

"Hi, it's me." Nick's voice was heavy with sleep.

"Hi, me, sorry for waking you up. I just needed to talk to my best mate."

"Hmm. Are you okay?"

Bridget could hear him yawning and stretching on the other end of the line.

"Yeah, I'm safe but just depressed and sick of myself. I'm so stupid, Nick."

"What happened?"

"I met this guy."

Nick moaned in exasperation. "What? A guy? Bridget, it has been three days since you left Jackson. Three days! You have no business getting involved with any guy for any reason right now. And then, realizing that he hadn't heard her out, his tone softened. "I'm sorry, I didn't give you a chance to explain, go ahead."

"No, you are right to be exasperated. I met a guy, a really nice guy, but I rushed things and he ended up staying the night. He didn't hurt me, it's not like he's a serial killer or anything, I just feel stupid for being so desperate and having no self-control." Her voice began to quiver with emotion. "I've forgotten what's good about me, Nick. I'm just sick of myself."

Nick didn't answer right away and when he did his voice was tender. "There's plenty that's good about you Bridget." But you have to learn how to be alone and happy before you can be with someone and be happy. There are good men out there, but you have to be willing to change your expectations. My mom always said that the best apples were at the top of the tree and the hardest ones to find and she was right." The silence on Bridget's end told Daniel she was crying. "You're the best friend I've ever had Bridget and I hate to see you sad. I think you're crazy sometimes, but I'll always be here for you. What are you going to do now? Will you come home?"

A part of Bridget wanted to go home, but she had left for a reason, to learn about herself and to reinvent herself where nobody had any preconceived notions about her. "No Nick. I'm going to find somewhere to settle up here and make a go of it. Thanks for listening to me, you're my bestie and I love you." Nick's voice was soft in reply. "I love you too."

Once Bridget was dressed, she went into Bluegum and bought some supplies, including a map of Queensland. Her motel room had been cleaned and the bed made when she returned. It matched her mood. She felt energized. It was finally time to leave her old life and her old mistakes behind her. But she needed a place to lay down roots. She spread the map out over the small circular dining table, holding it in place with the pepper and salt shakers on two corners and the sugar bowl on another. She rummaged in her shopping bag and ripped open a crackling plastic package containing a brand new red felt pen. She leaned close to locate Bluegum on the map and placed a small red dot there, then, raising the pen like a dagger, she shut her eyes and dropped her arm, randomly onto the map. It had landed about two inches away from the Bluegum dot. "Good, not too far to drive then," she muttered. She squinted and shifted her head to the side to see the name of her new hometown. Currawong about an hour away from Bluegum. She liked the name of the town immediately. Currawong, one of her favourite Australian birds, like a large black crow with patches of white on the tips of its wings was a good omen to her. She had no idea what was at Currawong, maybe she would arrive to find nothing, but she was going to go anyway and see what happened.

The trip was uneventful, but as she drew closer to her destination, she was pleased to see green fields, rather than the harsh yellow bushlands she had been expecting. A large sign on the side of the road said: "You are entering Currawong – pop 5000." She instantly felt like she had gone back 60 years. The houses were vintage weatherboard houses, circa 1950 with immaculate gardens and pristine driveways. Many of the homes were on acreage with a couple of horses grazing back from the road. The main strip was fairly modern but it only took a few minutes to drive through the center of town and then she was back out in the country.

Being careful to keep to the speed limit, she headed for the motel she had booked into back in Opal Bay. "Turn left in 100 meters," said the ever polite voice on her GPS. As Bridget turned left she admired a sweet old bluestone church on the corner. A group of parishioners were in the front weeding and tending the garden. They were an assorted group of moms, dads, children, teenagers and old age pensioners, all working together in a steady rhythm. With her windows rolled down, she could hear laughter and chatter coming from the group. Something inside her wished she could park the car and join in; there seemed to be such a spirit of belonging amongst them.

That night as she lay in her motel bed, looking through the newspaper for rental properties, she reflected on the little church again. As a little girl, her parents had taken her every week to church and she had enjoyed their time together as a family. She remembered the solemn feelings she held in her heart, even as a child, for the church and everything it stood for. She missed the reverent prayers, the quiet atmosphere, and the hope it all inspired. Maybe that was what was missing in her life? How far had she drifted away from her core beliefs? How much had she let the whims and wishes of others influence her away from what she held to be true? She made the decision there and then, that she would attend church services the next Sunday. Bridget felt much lighter over the next couple of days. She felt good about looking inside herself and facing her demons head on. It was nice to let the misery go and to commit to change. It felt like her soul was being washed clean in her resolve to be happy.

On Sunday morning, she dressed for church. Her packing had been abysmal with absolutely nothing that could pass as suitable for church, so the day before, she had bought herself a new dress befitting her mood. It was a crisp cotton dress with a fitted bodice and wide knee-length skirt in pale yellow. She matched it with a pair of summery slingback white stilettos and finished the look by pulling her auburn hair up into a long ponytail, making her look every bit as wholesome as she hoped she would. Looking herself over in the mirror she raised an eyebrow at her reflection. "This is it, Bridget. Don't let me down."

The walk to church seemed to be straight out of a Disney movie. The sun was shining, the birds singing, the breeze cool and refreshing. Families were walking to church together in their Sunday best. Bridget held back a little. She wanted to be the last to walk into the chapel so that she wouldn't be an object of curiosity to the others. At first, when she entered the chapel she was blinded in the cool dark after the brilliance of the outside sunshine. The chapel was nearly full friends and families in soft conversation, waiting for the reverend to emerge from the vestry. Bridget quietly took a seat in the last pew. Thankfully nobody had noticed her yet. She sat in quiet meditation, while the organist treated them to soft prelude music. It was rare that Bridget felt confident about one of her decisions, but today, she was convinced she was in the right place.

The prelude music faded and the congregation turned their faces in unison toward the vestry door. A soft click of a door latch at the side of the chapel released a beam of yellow light from within and emerging from the light, a tall figure, so tall and broad he had to bend his head to avoid hitting the top of the door. It was a blond head. From where she sat, Bridget couldn't see his face, only the back of his blond head and his black robes. Bridget's heart began to beat quicker. There was an uncomfortable sensation bubbling up from her stomach to her throat. The reverend was looking far too familiar for her liking. Then as the organist began to play the opening hymn, he turned around to face the congregation. Bridget took an audible gasp of air. Daniel! It was Daniel!

The congregation rose from their seats in a synchronized swoosh. Somewhere on the right side of the chapel, someone dropped their hymnbook with a loud clatter, but Bridget barely heard it; the chorus of voices around her was a muffled behind the blood whooshing through her ears. She felt faint and leaned forward to rest her head on the back of the pew in front of her. Daniel, a priest? Shame and anger threatened to drown her as she remembered with embarrassment their night together. If she'd known, she would have never.... How dare he not tell her? The shame began to dissipate. He was the one breaking his vows. She wasn't party to that. She looked up at him standing at the pulpit. Was he going to stand up there and preach from the Bible now?

The hymn ended and the congregation sat, waving fans in the heat, all eyes watching Daniel in rapt expectation. Bridget was glad that the chapel was full. It was unlikely that Daniel would see her sitting down in the back row, but leaving was out of the question; firstly, he would see her leave and think her a coward and secondly, she wanted to confront him. He started to speak and Bridget, in spite of herself was impressed. He wasn't preachy at all. He spoke of kindness and acceptance, service and dedication. He told amusing anecdotes that made the congregation chuckle, he mentioned people by name, he spoke of his own weaknesses. Bridget was starting to soften. Maybe the night with her was a one-off? Maybe, like everyone else, he had weaknesses that he was trying to work through? As the hour passed, so did her indignation. She gazed at Daniel. He was beautiful she had to admit. Maybe there could be a future with him? If she were to approach him and if he were willing, they could start afresh, and she would never ask him to overstep the boundaries of his faith. Nick's words nagged at her conscience, "you have to learn to be alone." "Oh, shut up, Nick," she mumbled out loud, making the people in front of her turn and stare.

After the service, Bridget, made her way against the stream of people leaving the chapel, up towards the pulpit, where Daniel was tidying up and preparing to leave. She arrived at the front just as he was heading towards the vestry.

"Reverend Inglis?"

Daniel turned swiftly with a ready smile, which fell comically as soon as he recognized her. "Yes? Oh!"

"Surprised to see me?"

Daniel's face froze into a stiff smile, but his eyes were boring into hers heavy with meaning. He spoke in urgent tones through his stiff smile like a ventriloquist. "Can't talk now." He glanced over Bridget's shoulder at someone approaching from behind. And then she heard the sound that made her blood run cold; a little girl's voice over the din of the departing congregation.

"Daddy!"

Like an ax dropping onto the executioner's block, Bridget's expression dropped into one of quiet fury. Not this. There would be no forgiving for this! She looked over her shoulder to see a little girl of about four, with honey colored curls running toward Daniel. He stood stiffly as his daughter hugged his legs. Following the little girl was a dark haired woman with a babe in arms. The woman approached her with a friendly smile. "Hello, you must be new? I'm Carrie Inglis, welcome!" She offered her hand to Bridget who did her best to hitch a believable looking smile onto her face. Whatever had happened was not this woman's fault, and she was not going to do anything that could possibly hurt her any further. "Hi, Carrie, nice to meet you."

Carrie's face was open, gazing directly into Bridget's eyes. "It's always good to have new people join us," she turned to Daniel, "isn't it honey?" But Daniel was already half way out of the chapel with his little girl in tow. Carrie laughed. "What's his rush? He's usually hanging around talking for ages after church. So, tell me about yourself, where are you staying?" She was so genuine that Bridget found herself wavering between shock and anger at Daniel and an irresistible connection with his wife. Overriding these two emotions was an overwhelming desire to get away, to be alone where she could lick her wounds and somehow come to terms with what had happened. She jotted down her address and phone number for Carrie and then making her excuses she made her way back to the motel room. It wasn't until she was alone that the full impact of what Daniel had subjected her to hit her. All of the excuses she had tried to make for him, fell flat and lifeless. He was a liar and a cheater and cheating on one of the loveliest ladies she had ever met and only a few weeks after she'd given birth to a new baby!

Like the voice of her conscience sitting on her shoulder, Nick's voice came to her mind. "It takes two to tango," he was saying, "Daniel didn't do this on his own."

"But I didn't know he was married!" she cried out to the room at large. "Did you know anything about him before you invited him home?" came Nick's steady voice again.

Bridget looked at her phone. If she had Nick's voice berating her in her head, she may as well call him and get the confession over and done with. He was going to find out about this at some point anyway, and she really needed his advice. When he answered his voice was cautious but hopeful.

"Hey Bridget, is this call to just say hi to your best friend because you miss me, or have you got bad news?"

Bridget sighed. "Bad news. He is a priest. A married priest with two children."

"Who, what? No, not the guy from the other night? How do you know?"

"I randomly attended his church today. How's that for serendipity?"

There was silence on the line for a moment. "Maybe serendipity, or maybe a life lesson? Maybe a chance to make things right? Wow, Bridge' what a shock. What's his wife like? Did she find out?"

"She's an absolute darling. Anybody who could willingly hurt a person like her has got to have something wrong with them, and no, thankfully, she doesn't know anything."

"What are you going to do?"

Bridget asked herself the same question. What was she going to do? She felt she had been directed to this little town, and directed to the church. Should she let Daniel's presence influence her own journey? No, why should he have a say? Maybe Currawong had happier surprises up its sleeve for her. The decision formed and settled in her heart. "I'm going to stay," she answered.

The week that followed was a blur. Carrie contacted her on the Tuesday with a fabulous rental opportunity. An elderly aunt and uncle were going overseas for six months and needed a house-sitter. The situation was perfect, she wouldn't have to buy furniture, the rent was cheap and the house boasted a backyard shady with glorious, mauve, Jacarandas and a wrap-around veranda, perfect for entertaining or working on her laptop. By Thursday she had moved in and made friends with neighbors and been invited for tea. By 10 o'clock that evening she was brushing her teeth getting ready for bed and feeling appreciative and hopeful for the future.

She had just pulled on an old t-shirt and a pair of Jackson's old boxers when she heard what she thought was a quiet knock on the front door. She stopped and cocked an ear to listen. Who would be knocking this late? The neighbor's dog started to bark. Bridget mentally retraced her going-to-bed ritual, had she locked all the doors? Confident that she had, she sank down onto her bed.

There it was again. Someone was definitely knocking. Padding silent as a cat in her bare feet, she approached the front door. She let out a sigh, grateful that she had taken the time to slip the safety chain into place. Another quiet knock, this time, more urgent than the last. Bridget pressed her face against the spy hole and switched on the porch light. Daniel's face, nervous and handsome was there, staring straight at the keyhole.

Jerking her face back, Bridget took a moment to decide what to do. What on earth could he want? She imagined he probably wanted to come to beg her to stay quiet about their night together. What a creep! In one swift movement, she had yanked the door open, the safety chain stopping it from opening further than four inches.

"What are you doing here?" She peered at him through the gap with narrowed eyes.

Daniel's smile was sheepish. "Bridget, I was hoping we could talk?"

"What about?"

"Us." He tried to stare seductively through the small gap in the doorway. He looked like an idiot. "I can't forget our night together, can you?" When she said nothing, he continued. "Can I come in? I'm feeling a bit exposed here under the porch light."

Bridget couldn't believe the brazen cheek of the man. "I've got nothing to hide, Daniel, and there isn't any 'us' as you put it." Her words were as sharp as razor blades. "And you've got a bloody cheek coming here and expecting me to be complicit in hurting a beautiful person like Carrie! I'm not in the business of dating married men and even if you don't appreciate your beautiful family, I do. Now rack off, before I call Carrie and tell her everything!" She slammed the door, breathing deeply with anger. Perhaps she should tell Carrie. She didn't deserve to be treated with this kind of callous, disrespect. She deserved to be rid of Daniel. Bridget imagined with satisfaction, Carrie confronting Daniel and kicking him out on the street. But there in the background of her fantasy was a small four-year-old girl crying and a baby who would only ever know weekend visits from his father.

The picture was so sad; she knew that she would never tell. She refused to add to her list of regrets, the destruction of a family.

She didn't hear from Daniel again. In spite of the drama, Bridget felt that Currawong was going to be good for her. It filled her with pride to face her fears, to confront her weaknesses and direct her attention to the needs of others for a while. Carrie was showing her that. Every day, in one way or another, Carrie was doing something to help. It didn't matter if it was a human need or a stray animal, everyone who needed it, got a dose of her kindness and attention. It inspired Bridget to do the same.

The wet season hit Queensland earlier than usual and out of the blue. One afternoon, a couple of weeks after moving in, Bridget sat in her study, staring at the torrential downpour outside. The power was out, there was no TV, and the battery on her laptop was flat and it looked like she would be forced to indulge in a lazy afternoon curled up on the couch with a book. Her phone rang. On the other end, she could hear Carrie over the din of the rain. It sounded like she was inside a tin shed. Carrie was shouting, but Bridget could only catch intermittent words. "Help – deliver shopping – old – car- time?"

Bridget yelled back. "I couldn't really hear what you said, but if you need my help, come and get me. I'll be waiting at my place!" Bridget caught a muffled "Thanks!" and hung up the phone. Fifteen minutes later, she was in the front seat of

Carrie's car in a yellow raincoat. "Okay, what am I helping you with today?"

Carrie grabbed Bridget's hand and squeezed it. "You're an angel for coming. I just need to deliver these meals to some elderly shut-ins today. Their usual delivery service is canceled due to the rain and I couldn't bear it if they went without a meal or a friendly face today. With your help, I'll be able to get it done in half the..." A loud screeching of wheels forced them to turn in terror to their right. A truck had lost control and was sliding from the opposite lane directly into their path. Before the truck slammed into them, Bridget caught a glimpse of the desperate expression on the face of the other driver. And then there was nothing.

She was in the strange house with the corridors again. This time, there was pain. Bridget resisted. She didn't want to have this dream but have it she would. Stretching away into the distance the corridor elongated. The doors came into view, beckoning her to start searching for that elusive something. She tried to grip the walls but her hands slid off, slick and wet. Against her will, she found herself at the first door. I'm running out of time... out of time... Someone was calling her from far away, "Bridget!" they called. I can't find you! She was rummaging through the room, searching. "Bridget!" The voice was louder now, from somewhere nearby, "Please wake up!" She was frantic. Help me find you!

Bridget felt herself emerge from the coma as though traveling an elevator one floor at a time. When she got to the top, her eyes opened. All around her were blurred moving shapes and muffled sounds. Only one shape directly in front of her face stayed still. She focused on it and waited for the blurriness to go away. Gradually, the shape became more distinct, the lines sharper, it was a face. It was Nick's face, wet with tears and he was smiling. Suddenly his face was next to hers and he was sobbing. She didn't know why. But now that Nick was there, everything was going to be all right.

Nick was there every day over the next two weeks in the hospital. Bridget had a concussion, a few broken ribs, a collapsed lung and her spleen had been removed. Nick told her that she had been in a coma for three days after the accident. He had taken the first flight to Queensland and had been by her side ever since. Carrie hadn't fared so well. She was still in a coma in intensive care with multiple broken bones and a head injury.

On her day of discharge, Bridget made her way to Carrie's hospital room. Daniel was by her bedside. His face was white. He looked at Bridget with eyes frantic and bloodshot. She realized in an instant that he was already receiving his punishment, nothing she could say could make him feel worse than he did right now. So, he loved his wife after all; or was this just guilt? Perhaps it was not her place to judge. She took a few ginger steps into the room and gripped the bars at the foot of Carrie's bed.

"How is she?"

Daniel leaned his elbows on the bed and rested his face in his hands. "Not good."

"I think we may have both learned the same lesson from this experience, Daniel. Since I met Carrie I've been judging you for taking your wife for granted. But I now realize that I've been taking someone for granted too, someone who has loved me my whole life and has watched and waited patiently while I've repeatedly thrown myself at people who didn't hold a candle to him. Buddha once said, 'The trouble is; you think you have time,' well now we both know that everything that is important can be taken in an instant. There is no time to waste, we only have now." Bridget turned to go and then hesitating she murmured without looking back. "Take care Daniel, I'll keep you and Carrie in my prayers."

The sunshine was bright in her hospital room when she walked stiffly through the door. Nick had his back to her; he was packing her pajamas and underwear into a duffle bag. Bridget eased her sore body into the chair by the bed and watched him. His big hands were awkward as he fumbled with her silky underwear. His brow was furrowed, his honest, open eyes, tense with the effort, his upturned boyish nose wrinkled in determination. From under her ribs, a wave of peace and security flooded her, filling her up until her heart felt like it would burst. She let out a delighted laugh. Why hadn't she been able to see it before? All the years of pain and misery looking for Mr. Right when she had the perfect man right under her nose the whole time. "I love Nick." Saying it to herself made it all the truer. She loved Nick and when the time was right she would tell him.

"There, he said with finality, zipping up the duffle bag. Where would you like to go next, my lady?"

"Home, please, Nick," she answered, rising to her feet. "Take me home."

AMISH CREEK

MONICA MARKS

59

Winter

The night had taken on a cold chill and it was somehow fitting of the heaviness in Jacob's heart. He gently urged the horses forward as they shied from an oncoming car, carefully guiding them closer to the ditch at the side of the road. Ahead of his carriage were two more, one for each of his brothers and their respective wives. The family was approaching the market and Jacob was grateful for his hands were slowly freezing against the reins despite the heavy woolen gloves covering them. The three carts eased into the wide parking area to the left of the treeline and Eliza, Jacob's younger sister-in-law, was the first out of carriage, already busying herself with the merchandise in the back of the wagon. By the time Jacob pulled his horses to a full stop, she had managed to unload a substantial number of goods. She smiled briefly at him as he approached to assist her but waved him away.

"It's all right, Jacob, I am quite capable of handling this here. You can go about whatever you need to do in your carriage." Jacob nodded but said nothing. He had never been one to say much.

"That's why you're not married," Jonah would tease him. "The women have no idea what you're thinking. How are they supposed to know that you have marriage on your mind when you say so little?" Jonah had no way of knowing how his words upset Jacob as it was merely meant to be brotherly teasing but Jacob often wished that he was more outspoken. Yet when he was in the presence of his female peers, he found himself more tongue-tied than usual. Gabriel and Jonah often pointed out the blue painted gates of the eligible women in town but Jacob always averted his eyes and changed the subject or maintained complete silence. Eliza and Jonah had just wed the previous month and as his just barely younger brother hopped down to join his new wife, Jacob could not help but feel a pang of envy at the new scruff covering his sibling's face. Subconsciously, Jacob found himself touching his own clean shaven, soft cheek, wondering if he would ever be able to boast the beard of a married man.

"Come along now, Jacob," Gabriel urged suddenly appearing at his side. "The cheese will freeze if you stand here too long."

"Really, Jacob," Louisa scowled. "You know better than to stand there while our goods go bad." At the sound of his older sister-in-law's voice, Jacob shifted his eyes downward and picked up the pace of unpacking the freshly churned cheese onto the wheelbarrows Eliza had dug out from the depth of her cart. Louisa was the dark, complete opposite of Jonah's sweet natured, cheerful mate. Louisa was only a year older than Jacob but she looked and acted like Jacob's ninety-year-old grandmother. She was starch and rigid and unlike Jacob's beloved grandmother, never had a kind word to say. Jacob could never understand why his older brother, Gabriel had married such an embittered woman. Gabriel was without a doubt the most attractive and hardest working member of their family. He was mild mannered and intelligent and he could have had his pick of any number of eligible women in their community. However, that was neither here nor there at that moment as Louisa's look of anger was deepening by the second as she watched Jacob's idling. Gabriel took the wheelbarrow from Jacob's hands, also noticing the look on Louisa's face and followed Jonah and Eliza toward the indoor market, Jacob close behind them, Louisa on his heels like a rabid sheepdog trying to keep in in line. Once inside, Jacob was relieved for the wood burning stoves which were filled with fresh wood and already warming the giant barn, despite the early morning hour. Someone had taken care to ensure the vendors were comfortable upon their arrival. It was barely six o'clock and the winter sun had yet to break through the blackness of night but the smell of the wood against cold winter air brought a surge of familiar melancholy to Jacob. He had been feeling lost the past few months, as if he were missing a key element, like air or water. He suspected that Jonah's wedding had helped bring about the sudden loneliness. *You need to find a wife and start a family. You're twenty-five years old. You are the last man in the family and you're unmarried. Even your younger brother is married before you! That is shameful!* Louisa's sharp tone snapped him out of his brooding.

"Are you going to stand there until the sun goes down, Jacob?" He shuffled forward without looking up, joining the rest of his family at their booth. He liked this venue. It was a true Amish market, lit with soft gaslights and no electricity. It had once been an old, neglected barn belonging to a vast colonial house but years after the family who had owned it went bankrupt, the land was distributed among the Amish communities evenly. The house had been demolished and Jacob's family lived on one part of the fruitful farmland, raising goats, cows and chickens. They had been dairy farmers for generations. A neighboring district had reconstructed the dilapidated barn, expanding it to four times its size and they had created a small trader's market within the grand structure. Everyone was welcome, provided they respected the land. On any given day from Tuesday to Saturday, there were merchants selling jams and quilts, sweaters and meats. Only the freshest vegetables and cheeses could be found in the simple wooden booths, packed in ice and metal buckets. Once in a while, a more ambitious traveler would set up a crate boasting homemade wine or cider but those peddlers were becoming more and more scarce as the demand for their supply diminished. While it was open to the general public, it maintained the virtue in which Jacob was raised and he felt more at home at this particular location than any of the others at which they frequented over the year. Their cheeses were on display in a very short time and now there was little else to do but wait for traffic. Eliza immediately sat upon a skid of wood and began knitting while Louisa seemed content to stand back, arms folded and tight lipped, sternly watching the vendors prepare to the upcoming day.

"Did you bring something to read, Jacob?" Eliza asked brightly, smiling at him. Jacob nodded quickly and lowered his blue eyes, blushing. Her smile widened but she did not tease him. Jonah, however, seized the opportunity.

"We are ever so grateful that you did, Jacob! Otherwise you might never stop talking!" Jacob reached into his burlap sack to remove a book he had recently borrowed from the library in Lancaster, ignoring his brother.

"Leave him alone," Gabriel growled at Jonah. "At least he knows when to stay quiet."

"Oh, quiet yourself, Gabriel. If I can't tease Jacob, who can?"

"No one needs to bother Jacob," Eliza piped in pleasantly. "I think it's wonderful that he has such a disposition. It will take him far in life."

Jacob almost hugged his new sister. Instead he offered her a timid smile before looking back down at the pages before him.

"No one needs to be silent all the time," Louisa retorted. "Really, Jacob, how are you going to court anyone without learning how to speak?"

"That's enough!" Gabriel snapped. Everyone looked at him in surprise, including Jacob. "Jacob will marry when the time is right and he will speak to someone when he finds someone worthy of hearing his voice. Now leave him be!" Inexplicably, tears sprung into Jacob's eyes. Jonah looked abashed while Louisa looked contrite.

"Of course," Louisa mumbled, retreating to her spot against a post. Gabriel drew close to his younger brother.

"There is nothing wrong with you. You are patient, kind and you will make a just minister to our district one day. Don't let anyone tell you otherwise."

"Thank you, brother," Jacob murmured. Gabriel patted him reassuringly on the shoulder and went to join his wife. Jacob watched him walk away and wondered if that speech of confidence was actually for him or if Gabriel was just thinking to himself aloud.

The day got colder even as the sun fought to break through the ominous clouds. A storm was brewing and the market was suffering as a result. Only a few people had dared venture out as the temperatures dropped to a desolate, inconsolable place. It was the kind of day where even the marrow of the bones was chilled and could not be warmed under any circumstance. Most of the patrons were tourists passing through Amish country but a few neighboring communities stopped by to provide their support. Jacob was happy he had thought to bring along another book as he had barely had occasion to raise his eyes from the first one he had packed. Then fate mysteriously intervened.

It started as a shriek. Startled, Jacob looked up and blinked as an object came hurling at his head. Out of nowhere, a body slammed into his and he was belly down under the neighboring booth, Gabriel on top of him. A peal of child's laughter rang out, followed by a group chuckle and it was clear that whatever had occurred had merely been the act of a clumsy or mischievous child. But as Jacob rose put his hands down to raise his body up, his eyes locked upon a pair of light brown irises, crouched down like a preying tiger directly at his level. There was a face inches from his underneath the table, their lips almost touching one another. And suddenly Jacob was not in the din of the market any longer.

They skipped in a circle, the long grasses tickling their knees as the group picked up speed. The scent of wildflowers and herbs filled the air. Jacob's head was feeling light and he wasn't sure if it were as a result of the dizzying game or the beautiful eyes of his classmate, Grace which seemed to be fixated on his own. Even at the tender age of eight, Jacob recognized the impossible beauty of those orbs, a luminous, liquid brown, so light they seemed gold in the springtime sunlight. The round dance continued a few more laps until Grace herself "tripped" and landed the group into an unceremonious pile of young, panting bodies onto the lea. Yet through the reeds, Grace still stared at him and he at her. And not once did he feel the urge to look away in shyness.

"Jacob!" the eyes spoke. Quickly, Jacob lifted his head to stand and hit his skull against the booth, creating a sickening crack at the impact. His hand raised instinctively to his head.

"Oh! Are you all right?" She was at his side, grabbing his arm in aide. Jacob was immediately torn. He knew that he was not supposed to have this kind of contact with an outsider but this outsider was different...she was Grace.

"Uh...yes, thank you. Hello Grace," he mumbled, staring up at her. "How are you?"

Grace smiled that off-centered, charming grin which could disarm the angriest of bees.

"I'm well, Jacob. I'm so happy to see you here! I have been here a few times in the last months but you are never here when I come. I have been yearning for your goat cheese for years now and I finally had the courage to come around. Have you any for sale? Truly you can't find anything like your family's cheeses in the city."

Jacob nodded and before he could lead her around to the booth, he was looking up directly into Louisa's scowling face.

"Come along, Jacob," Louisa intervened, pulling him from Grace. "You're needed."

"But she wants – "Jacob protested.

"Eliza can help her," Louisa snapped. "Eliza! Help this woman!"

Louisa almost spat the word "woman" as she scathingly glared at Grace. Grace looked forlorn as she watched his sister-in-law shuffle him away. She slowly raised a gloved hand and smiled sadly as he looked back at her.

"Bye Jacob," she mouthed.

"You should know better, Jacob," Gabriel chided. They were back in their home, gathered by the warm hearth of the fire, counting their profits from the day. Jonah and Eliza looked up questioningly.

"Oh do tell! What could our patient Jacob possibly have done to earn trouble?" Eliza joked. "This I must hear!"

"Your brother-in-law was fraternizing with a fallen woman, a shunned member of this community," Louisa snapped. "Looking after her like some lost lamb. You should be ashamed of yourself, Jacob! You are just asking for trouble!"

"Who?" Eliza and Jonah chorused. "Which shunned woman?"

"That Beiler woman," Gabriel replied quietly. Eliza's eyes lit up.

"Lydia?" she squealed. "Oh how is she?"

Louisa's frown deepened into her characteristic scowl.

"No, the other one. Grace. Their poor, shamed parents. Can you imagine? Having two of your children living scandalously in the city? What are the odds of that occurring? It's no surprise they're in such poor health."

"Jacob, you saw Grace today?" Naomi, Jonah's twin looked up from kneading bread to address her younger brother. "How did she look? Is she well?"

Jacob nodded. Naomi and Grace had been very close before Grace had left the church. Naomi had been devastated when Grace had been exiled and she had never completely recovered. Probably no more than Jacob had.

"She said she was well," Jacob replied.

"You spoke to her?" their father was incensed from his rocking chair at the hearth. "Jacob, I expect better from you!"

"She was there to buy cheese!" Gabriel jumped in. "You cannot make a sale if you do not speak with the customers, papa."

Jacob looked gratefully at his brother.

"In the future, you let the women handle the women," their father muttered. All the siblings exchanged a secret smile, except, of course, Louisa.

"Jacob, what a pleasant surprise. How are you?" The bishop looked up from a pile of papers and smiled at the man in his doorway. "Please come in."

"Hello, Bishop. Is this an opportune time?"

"Of course! I don't get to see enough of you. Oh! Wait! I know what this is about! You're here to announce a betrothal!" The heavy set man clapped his hands together, his eyes lighting up with happiness. "Who is the lucky woman?"

Jacob shook his head quickly and averted his expressive blue eyes.

"No, Bishop. It's not a marriage announcement..." The bishop read Jacob's somber expression and his smile faded. He gestured at a simple chair across from his desk.

"Please sit down," he encouraged the younger man. Jacob obliged, still staring at the floor.

"Is something wrong, Jacob?"

"No...well..." Jacob paused, unsure of how to word what he wanted to say. He wished he had asked Gabriel for advice before doing something this inane. If his father found out...well it was too late now.

"Bishop, if someone were to be excommunicated, could they ever come back?" Sighing, Bishop Fisher sat back against the rigid chair and pushed his spectacles off the bridge of his nose, onto his receding hairline.

"Jacob, the idea behind rumspringa is for you to see what waits for you beyond the security of our community. That is why we look the other way when the young people go and experiment with different aspects of the world in which we don't engage before making the very important choice of being baptized. Once you are baptized, we expect that you have 'sowed your wild oats' so to speak. So Jacob, if you are having a crisis of faith, we can help you through community and prayer but if you choose to leave the Amish community now, it will be very difficult for you to return. Realistically, I would say nearly impossible. "

Jacob laughed, startling the man.

"I'm sorry, Bishop. I didn't mean to laugh. You needn't worry about me. I have no desire to go anywhere away from my family and land. I was asking about someone else." The bishop looked slightly more relaxed but curiosity gleamed in his eye.

"Could you give me the circumstances?" he asked. Jacob suddenly realized his mistake. The community was too close. There was no possible way that this meeting would not reach the ears of his family. He was acting like a foolish child, making this trip and asking ridiculous questions. Why would he assume that Grace would ever want to come back? She most likely loved her life in the city. She and may even be married already! Shame stained his cheeks crimson and Jacob stood suddenly.

"I'm sorry, Bishop. This was a silly thing for me to do. I made a mistake." Without waiting for an answer, Jacob hurried out of the small house and down the road toward his farm.

Jacob was about to vomit. He could feel the bile raising to his mouth, creating a pool of saliva under his tongue. *Don't get ill! You foolish, foolish man! What are you doing here?*

An elderly woman smiled kindly at him and handed him a paper bag from beside her seat.

"Motion sickness, honey?" she asked. Tentatively, Jacob accepted the bag. Then, to his horror, he retched into it. Surprisingly, after he was finished, he felt much better. The aging woman nodded knowingly.

"There you go. My grandson gets carsick too. He's only ten but I carry bags just in case. I didn't think people got carsick at your age," she told him.

"I've never been on a bus before," Jacob admitted. Her grinned widened and she nodded understandingly, taking in his simple, homespun clothing.

"Well that would explain it then. Just take deep breaths and try to relax. We'll be in Philadelphia in less than an hour." Jacob nodded and tried to heed her advice but his stomach would not settle. He imagined that had more to do with what he was doing than the actual bus ride itself. This was completely out of character for him. In fact, he could hardly believe what he was doing. He didn't know what he was hoping to accomplish but he also knew that since the day he had seen Grace in the market, he had been unable to think of anything but her. Her heart-warming smile was in the fireplace, her dark honey eyes were in the rays of sunlight streaking through the pines. He heard her voice in the chirping birds and once he thought he even saw her standing behind their barn but of course it had only been his mind playing tricks. He could not get her out of his head. He had to know if she was happy, if she thought of him or at least if she missed her life and her family in the district. Of course what he was doing was forbidden and if he were caught, he would be punished. But that would be the least of his problems. He would never hear the end of it from Louisa. Yet none of that seemed to matter. He would not rest until he knew that Grace was happy in her life. Even if that meant she was content without him.

As the older woman had predicted, less than an hour later, the bus was pulling into the hectic station in Philadelphia. Jacob had never seen such chaos. During rumspringa, he and Jonah had gone into town twice. Jonah had put on outsider clothing, smoked a cigarette and drank beer. Jacob had almost been sick from all of the foreign smells and the bustle. While he had accompanied his brother, he never felt the need to experiment with anything he did not know. There had never been any doubt that Jacob would be baptized. Unlike his peers, he had never felt the need go outside of is upbringing to see how good was their life. He recognized the purity in their way, the unity they had with nature and with each other. He couldn't imagine a life without the structural peace in which he had been reared. Jacob had always felt blessed by his birthright and respected the culture immensely. It was for all of these reasons that his underarms were soaked in perspiration at that moment, despite the crisp winter air. He nodded good-bye to his bus mate and slowly walked off the vehicle, his head swimming from all of the activity. *Stay focussed on your task, Jacob. You will be home before anyone realizes you are gone.* Once off the bus, he reached into the pocket of his plain brown pants and withdrew a scrap of paper. Then looking about, he spotted a taxi cab stop on the outskirts of the bustling station. Without hesitation, he made his way into a car and muttered the address written on the piece he was holding. The cabbie raised his eyebrow slightly at the sight of his passenger but made no comment at Jacob's outdated clothing.

"Is this your first time in Philly?" the man asked pleasantly, somehow feeling the need to put his obviously uncomfortable fare at ease. Jacob nodded quickly but stared out the window. His head was beginning to ache from all of the sights and sounds whizzing by the window.

"There's a lot of history here," the driver offered but when Jacob did not reply, he gave up and continued the relatively short trip to his destination. Jacob paid the charge and nodded before climbing onto the sidewalk. As the car drove away, he found himself looking back at the paper and then up at the apartment which he faced. He was in the right spot according to the phone book he had consulted at the Lancaster Library. This was Grace's home. For a moment, he considered aborting the mission all together and running back to the safety of Lancaster County. *But then you'll never know,* he told himself. And that was all the convincing he needed. He started up the steps and was inside the tiny entranceway, looking for her name on the intercom system. A teen boy walked out of the lobby and held the door open so Jacob slipped inside, rather than searching for the code. The phone book had declared Grace's apartment to be 401. Jacob opted for the stairs rather than the elevator. He reached the fourth floor and knocked on the door boasting 401 in scarred gold numbers. After a moment, he heard footsteps and a woman sing out.

"Coming!" Jacob swallowed and tried to prepare himself for coming face to face with the only woman who he had been able to speak with his entire life. But when the door flew open, it was not Grace. In Jacob's intense disappointment, he almost walked away, not realizing that he was looking at Lydia, Grace's younger sister.

"Jacob Miller! I don't believe my eyes!" she hollered. "Grace! You won't believe who is at our door!"

Jacob turned back to the doorway he was already departing, his eyes filled with hope at the sound of Grace's name.

"Is Grace here?" he asked, his voice no higher than a whisper. Lydia nodded eagerly and ushered him into the tiny apartment. Seconds later, Grace appeared in the hallway, her lava-like eyes wide with surprise.

"It really is you, Jacob! What – how...oh don't tell me you've been excommunicated!" Grace cried, rushing forward to embrace him in a hug. Not wanting to move but willing himself to do so, he stepped out of her friendly gesture and shook his head, color blushing his face with embarrassment.

"No...I...I came to see you, Grace," he said. "Is there any way we can speak? Just for a few moments?"

Lydia looked shocked but quickly nodded and said she was on her way out. She picked up a set of keys from the kitchen table and smiled briefly before flying out the door. Before she closed the door, she turned to Jacob, her eyes shiny.

"I understand that your brother wed Eliza Lapp. Please, if you find it in your heart, can you tell Eliza I think of her often?" Lydia did not wait for an answer and Jacob realized it was because she was about to cry. The door to the apartment closed and Grace smiled welcomingly at Jacob.

"Please, come and sit down. Can I offer you anything? A tea?" Jacob shook his head and sat down on the edge of an old velvet sofa.

"I can't tell you how wonderful it is to see you! I haven't been able to stop thinking about you since I saw you last week. I have been trying to find covert ways to see you and Naomi since I left. This has been my only fruitful attempt thus far. How is your sister?

Jacob nodded.

"She is well. She heard that I had seen you and asked the same. I believe she misses you very much, Grace." She smiled sadly.

"I miss her also. And I miss you, Jacob. You were my very first love." Jacob was stunned to hear the words. He had hoped, maybe even suspected that Grace had thought of him lovingly but he had always been far too bashful to find out if she held the same types of feelings for him. He felt like a weight had been lifted off his chest, a barbell which had resided upon him since the horrible day that Grace had left his life.

"Why don't you come back?" he asked her seriously. "Do you want to come back?"

Grace sat heavily back against the rocking chair in which she sat.

"Very much, Jacob but it is not that simple. If Lydia wanted to return, she would have a much easier time of it. She was never baptized so in theory, she never really left the church. She's basically on an extended rumspringa. I, on the other hand, have been baptized and I turned my back on my vows to our community."

"Why did you leave?" Jacob pressed before he could stop himself. He wasn't sure he wanted to hear the answer. He had always feared that she had fallen in love with an outsider. Grace's face fell.

"When Lydia began her rumspringa, it was just about a year after you and I had been baptized. Justine and Joseph had just gotten married and it was only Lydia and I left in the house with our parents. The workload doubled and I was fine with that but Lydia had always been willful. She began to act out and refuse to do the work. My parents' health had begun to fail at that point.

Suddenly, Lydia was not coming home at night and I would go looking for her and find her in cars with boys, high off marijuana, wearing skimpy clothing. I was only grateful my mother never had to witness anything of the sort or she would surely be dead by now of a heart attack. Night after night, I would drag Lydia home, pour cold water on her head and sober her up but this wasn't just a phase. I knew she was going to leave." Grace paused and looked up at Jacob.

"She is my little sister, Jacob. She is lost and naïve and doesn't know the ways of the world. She needed someone to protect her. She had no one..."

Jacob felt a lump grow in his throat. Grace was such an incredible sister. Would he do the same thing for Jonah or Naomi? He was ashamed but he knew that he would not. It took courage to do what she did for Lydia.

"How is Lydia doing now?" Jacob asked. He feared the answer.

"She is wonderful! She went to college and got a degree as a paralegal. She met a very nice man, a lawyer and I do believe he is going to propose any day now." Grace smiled but Jacob read the pain in her eyes.

"Do you want to come home?" Jacob asked again. Grace nodded slightly but changed her affirmative into a shrug.

"That's really not relevant, Jacob. I won't be welcomed back. I have learned to accept that fact. I knew what I was doing and this is my penance for making such a choice."

"You must speak to Bishop Fisher, Grace!" Jacob told her. She shook her head.

"You must go back home, Jacob and forget about me. If anyone finds out you were here..." She rose and went to guide him to the door.

"I can't tell you how wonderful it is to see you, Jacob. If you somehow find a way, tell your sister I miss her dearly. But don't put yourself into any trouble doing so." Instinctively, she reached out and embraced Jacob. Before he could stop himself, he had wrapped his own arms around her and relished the feeling of her closeness for one blissful moment. It might be the last time he ever had the opportunity.

"Good-bye, Jacob," she whispered in his ear and slowly closed the door, leaving him staring at it, troubled and confused.

"Bishop, is this an inopportune time?"

"Jacob! You left so quickly the other day, I thought it was something I had said!" the jovial man rose quickly from behind the scarred desk and hurried to greet Jacob at the door. "Please come in!"

Jacob moved further into the small office and sat before the elder, choosing his words carefully.

"Have you come to further discuss what we started the other day?" Jacob nodded.

"Sir, do you recall the Beiler sisters? Grace and Lydia?" The man frowned deeply, apparently troubled by the mention of their names.

"Yes," he replied slowly. "Why do you ask?"

"Grace would like to come home," Jacob answered simply. The Bishop began to shake his head at once but for the first time in his life, Jacob felt a rod of steel fuse into his spine and he sat up straight in his chair. He would not take no for an answer. Not this time.

"I do not think that is in the realm of possibility, son," the kindly man said. "Now if Lydia wanted to rejoin us, that might be possible since she has yet to be baptized however, it would be a process – "

"Lydia is very happy living in the outside world. Grace knows her place is here with us." The bishop continued to shake his head and Jacob felt his jaw clench, a motion that was foreign and unsettling to both men. Bishop Fisher seemed to recognize his anger at once and tried to diffuse the situation with logic.

"Jacob, what you are asking is out of the question. Grace Beiler chose to leave after she already committed herself to us. She not only abandoned our community, she left her own family to contend with an awful burden from both a labor and personal standpoint. Surely you cannot ignore those facts!" Jacob stared defiantly at Bishop Fisher.

"You don't know all of the facts, Bishop or you would change your mind," Jacob almost spat between clenched teeth. "Grace Beiler is an honorable woman and she belongs here with her people. She is willing to repent and undergo whatever punishment you deem fit to allow her back but please, Bishop, you must consider this!" Again, the Bishop shook his head, his eyes misty with sadness.

"This is not my decision to make, Jacob. Grace already made the decision for herself. There is nothing I can do. You must forget about Grace Beiler. There are many eligible women who would be very fortunate to be wed to you, Jacob. Please try to focus on what is feasible.

Grace Beiler is a dream." The Bishop stood up, indicating the conversation was done. Jacob felt familiar the lead weight of loneliness overwhelm his chest. He had known that this was apt to be the end result but he would have never forgiven himself if he had not given it a sincere chance. But he had failed. And Grace would never be there to untie his tongue as she had in childhood. As he slowly let himself outside into the cold winter afternoon, he somehow didn't see Grace's eyes in the sunlight for the first time since their encounter at the market.

<u>Spring</u>

The first day of warmth was a time for celebration among the Miller family. Although the temperatures had just barely climbed above freezing, it was enough to have melted the snow and cause a slushy mess for children to stomp around while the men bravely retired their heavy wool coats and the women dared leave the wash on the line all day without fear of freezing the handmade fabrics. Even Louisa seemed to be in a good mood as the brand new baby buds dripped snowflakes into puddles of water and caught the golden sunrays in their reflections. Louisa had just discovered she was with child and for the first time that anyone could remember, she was actually smiling. It was a lovely smile, in fact and quite infectious. In fact, she often had kind words to say. The only one unaffected by the magic the season change appeared to bring about was Jacob. Not even Jonah and Eliza had been able to lift him out of the depth of his despair since his meeting with the Bishop. Of course Jacob had not disclosed the reason for his mood but instead thrown himself into work. When he was forced to be in the presence of others, he ensured he had a plethora of reading material at his side as to avoid any potential conversation. The day that the warmth finally remembered their district, Jacob had been up well before dawn, milking the cows as he always did. He wanted to be done the majority of his chores before retreating to the barn and hiding in the loft. He had actually acquired an interesting mystery from the library and he was eager to read the ending. As the morning hour turned close to noon, Jacob hurried out of the chicken coop with a basket full of eggs and almost slipped in the mud near the pig pen. Steadying himself before he lost the day's yolks, he grabbed onto the fence with his free hand and looked up. Directly on the other side of the gate was the most beautiful woman he had ever seen. Her long blonde hair was loose and hanging about her gray, ankle-length dress, under a matching gray bonnet, slightly blowing in the gentle breeze. Her mouth was turned up into a crooked smile, off centered but intensely charming and as it always did, sunlight caught the molten brown of her eyes, melting the sadness out of Jacob from the moment his forlorn irises met them.

"Grace!" he whispered, hushed and looked around figuratively. "What are you doing here?"

Her beam widened.

"This is my home, Jacob, and I've come to thank you for helping me find my way back. And also I would like to inform you that my parents have painted their gate blue."

Late Winter

No one could have prepared her for the man standing on the other side of the door but it truly was Bishop Fisher and he was there to speak to her. Lydia had conveniently disappeared, extremely uncomfortable by the reminder of the past she had left behind but Grace had welcomed the Bishop into the cozy apartment, offering him a hot tea and they had talked for hours, about Lydia, about her parents, about why she had left and of course, about Jacob. After their discussion, the Bishop told her that he wanted to have her return but he needed to discuss it with the ministers first. Of course, the process would be long and require intense atonement for what she had done. There was one more subtlety; that she would sincerely consider Jacob as a husband. Grace had smiled and nodded. After he left, she had shaken her head and laughed. How could the Bishop know that the main reason she had wanted to return for so many years was to be with Jacob?

ADA

Chapter 1

Ada looked at the letter she held in her hands. Her heart was beating hard. Part of herself was questioning the idea of even doing this. She was going to leave behind everything familiar, as terrible as it might be right now, for a man she had never met before. However, his letter and all his previous ones had looked kind enough.

"Ada,

It will be a pleasure to meet you. I have enjoyed conversing with you, and I will be waiting to meet you in the train station on the tenth of October. I hope you will have a safe journey.

Rainer"

While Rainer was usually a lot wordier, their letters had become shorter as they worked out the details of her travel.

"Dear God," Ada said, praying aloud as she finished packing her trunk. "I think you have really given me something special with Rainer. I pray that you would please help me have a safe journey and take away these fears that are plaguing me. Thank you for your mercy. Amen."

Ada sat on her bed as she stared at her trunk. It was not often that a women left a well settled Eastern town to go out West on the idea that they were going to marry a strange man, but Ada had always been one for adventure. Besides, leaving this town behind would let her leave her secret behind. There was no way it could follow her.

Ada took a deep breath. She would soon be able to leave everything behind. The trunk seemed to be full of everything she would need. She didn't even need to look around her room. It was completely empty. She had entered the house with only this trunk of things, and she had not had an opportunity to acquire any new belongings. Ada had already informed her landlady that she would be leaving. The woman had inquired about where she was going, but Ada had skirted around the answer. It was better that no one knew; her landlady tended to enjoy talking about the most interesting bits of news in regards to her tenants a bit too much for Ada's taste.

Ada smiled at the pile of letters she had from Rainer. They had been conversing over two months' time, and she felt as though she already knew him.

"Now, I just need to wait until my train leaves," Ada said, as the hours stretched before her. There would be no one to take leave of.

The next morning, Ada was happy to finally board the train. She had never been on a train before, and she was excited to see what it was like. She smiled to herself as she imagined what Rainer might look like. She had asked him to describe himself, but he only said that he had dark hair and dark eyes. Ada felt like her heart might recognize the man she had met through the letters. After all, if everything went well, they were to be married.

Ada's heart raced. Was she ready for marriage? She had to be. This was the only way to escape her hometown.

"Where are you going?" The woman sitting across from her asked amiably. Her voice startled Ada, and Ada put her hand over her heart.

"I'm sorry. I was completely distracted," Ada said. She smiled. "I'm going to Topeka, Kansas. And where are you going?"

"Denver, Colorado. My journey should be a fair bit longer than yours."

Ada smiled. "Are you visiting or moving?"

"Visiting," the woman nodded. "I grew up in Denver, but I wanted to move East when I got old enough to go out on my own."

Ada smiled. This woman had wanted to move East, and Ada had wanted to move West, each one escaping from where they had grown up. "I'm moving," Ada offered. "I grew up in. . . New York, but it was time for me to move on."

The woman smiled. "Well, I wish you good luck. Moving to a new part of the country can be a very difficult venture."

"Thank you," Ada said, her stomach rolling over. Perhaps it had been difficult for this woman, but anything would be better than her life in New York. She would finally be free to be herself and start over.

Ada passed the journey looking out the window and eating occasionally, but the hours stretched on. Ada felt as though she would never arrive in Topeka.

"What time should we arrive in Topeka?" she asked a man working on the train the next day.

"We are running a little behind schedule," the man said, glancing at his wristwatch. "I think we should arrive any time between four and five o'clock this evening."

Ada nodded. She hoped Rainer wouldn't mind waiting so long. She knew that she hated waiting, but at least when she was on the train, time seemed to pass more easily. However, her body was aching from spending the night sleeping in a sitting up position. Ada just wanted to arrive and sleep in a nice bed.

"I'm sorry," Ada said, stopping the same man as he made another round through the train. "What time is it?"

"1:30," the man replied.

Ada nodded. "Thank you." The time was passing more quickly than she had thought it would. Although lunchtime had already passed, Ada didn't feel the least tinges of hunger. She wondered how Rainer would act upon meeting her. Would he be affectionate right away or more cautious? Ada was naturally cautious, but she felt as though she already knew this stranger.

However, when it was time for Ada to deboard the train, what she saw was nothing like anything she had imagined.

Chapter 2

Ada scanned the crowd. She had never even seen a photo of this man. She assumed they did not have the kind of equipment out here in Topeka to even make a picture. However, there was one man in the crowd who just made her smile. He had dark hair, but Ada couldn't see his eyes. He was taller than a majority of the people.

Ada's heart fell as soon as she saw him talking to a woman. It couldn't be Rainer then. Ada took a deep breath and scanned the crowd again. She shouldn't be disappointed. Why was she disappointed? She had no right to feel disappointed just because Rainer wasn't the first handsome man she ran into.

There were two other men on one side who both had dark hair. One of them could easily be Rainer, but they weren't looking in her direction. Shouldn't they be looking for her? Was she supposed to approach random men and ask if they were named Rainer? This was ridiculous.

Ada let her eye wander back to that first man. He was looking right at her. He smiled and started striding over to her.

"Are you Ada?" he asked.

Ada's heart leaped, and the smile that popped onto her face was involuntarily. "Yes, I'm Ada. You must be Rainer then?"

The man nodded and awkwardly offered his hand. Ada felt strange shaking this man's hand like they had just made a business deal, but a hug would certainly not be appropriate at this time.

"It is such a pleasure to meet you," Rainer said. He looked down at her trunk. "Do you have any more things?"

"That's everything," Ada replied.

"Let's go then," Rainer said, turning and looking back. Ada saw that the woman she had first seen talking to Rainer was still standing there next to a pile of her things. Ada had assumed that Rainer was simply talking to her to find out if she was Ada. If that wasn't the case, why were there two women here for Rainer?

Ada wanted to ask, but she didn't feel comfortable enough yet. Instead, she asked a different question. "Where are we going?"

"I thought," Rainer said, turning back to look her full in the face. His face was chiseled and clean shaven. Ada liked the way he looked.

"I thought I would take you to my mother's house. She has offered you a place to stay. I just finished constructing my own cabin, but I don't think it's quite a home yet. I thought letting you stay in my mother and father's house would be a good place for you as we get to know one another."

Ada had heard horror stories about men who had met their women in the stations and married them that same day. Ada was glad that Rainer wanted to take his time. "I think it sounds very thoughtful of you to have planned this out," Ada said. She smiled up at him. "I'm ready to go with you."

Rainer scooped up Ada's suitcase and led her back over to the other woman.

"Ada, this is Kaya. Kaya, this is Ada."

"Pleased to meet you," Kaya said.

"You as well," Ada said, dropping a curtsy. Kaya stared at her strangely, and Ada wondered if her customs were out of place in this Western town. Ada desperately searched for a reason that this woman was going with them. Perhaps she was a family member. Rainer grabbed one of Kaya's bags, and she carried the smaller bag with her.

"I'll drop you off first, Kaya," Rainer said as he placed the suitcases in the back of his carriage. "Let me help you ladies up." Kaya bustled in to be let up first. Ada demurely followed behind. Rainer hoisted her up just as he had done for Kaya. He then went to the opposite side of the carriage and took the horses' reins. Kaya was in the middle.

Ada started becoming angry. She was supposed to be coming out to Topeka to meet a ranch owner who was free to marry. What then was this other woman doing here at the same time? Surely, Rainer had not been writing to more than one woman? Ada couldn't bear the thought. Returning to New York simply was not an option.

"How far do you live from the station?" Ada asked. She leaned forward a little so she could see Rainer around Kaya.

"It's not far. About half an hour's journey." Rainer immediately turned to Kaya. "The hotel is about ten minutes from here. I promise you that the owners are very friendly. I know them personally, and you will feel quite comfortable there."

Kaya smiled at Rainer, and Ada seethed. She was normally a very laid back person, but this woman was coming in and stomping all over her fairy tale. What was she supposed to do? Push Kaya out of the carriage and slide over next to Rainer? Ada shook her head and took a deep breath. She silently prayed and asked God for patience. She asked him for some of his mercy on this girl.

Ada felt a lot better after giving God her worries. The ride was short, and a few minutes later as the carriage rested on the edge of town, Rainer jumped out. He helped Kaya down then gathered her bags.

"I'll be right back. I'm just going to take these bags inside for Kaya. Will you be alright waiting here?"

Ada nodded, feeling the jealousy cropping up. Rainer started walking toward the hotel. Kaya stayed behind for a few minutes.

"Are you courting Rainer?" she asked in a low voice.

Ada paused. Were they courting? It was more like something more. They already knew they were going to get married. "Not exactly," Ada said, trying to explain. "I came to Topeka. I just met him, but. . ."

Kaya nodded. "Okay, I should probably go." She pointed at the hotel across the street. "Rainer is probably waiting."

But we're going to get married! Ada wanted to shout at Kaya, but Kaya was already bustling inside. Ada folded her arms and waited as the sun sank below the horizon. The sunset was beautiful, but Ada didn't enjoy it. She tried to reason with herself, but her idea of a happy ending seemed to be fast fading. She didn't want Kaya getting in her way, and she didn't know how long Kaya was planning to be here. Kaya's open question made her intentions clear enough.

Chapter 3

When Rainer got back in the carriage, all of the things that Ada wanted to say to him, warning him about Kaya's possible intentions were fading out of her mind. After all, even though she had come out here to marry Rainer, they might not fall in love. He might discover that their personalities were simply too different. After all, he didn't seem very picky or jealous like she was.

"Sorry about the delay," Rainer smiled at her. "I felt bad for her. She said that she didn't know how to find the hotel."

"Of course," Ada said. "It was kind of you to help someone you don't know at all." She emphasized those words to demonstrate the difference between herself and this new woman. "The sunset was beautiful."

Rainer smiled at her. "Isn't it? I love the way God puts a touch of beauty in everything he makes."

Ada smiled genuinely, feeling the stress seep away. "I agree. I'm glad that the countryside is so beautiful. While it is a far cry from what I know in New York, I somehow feel at home here."

"Perhaps it is because God created us to be at home no matter where we are in his world."

Ada liked the way that Rainer mentioned God and talked about him as though he was his best friend. "I know you have a lot of cows and few bulls from your letters," Ada said. "But I want to learn more about your farm." Ada sent him a sideways glance. She didn't have to feign interest. She already felt it strongly. "Tell about what you do every day. You're not confined to a small piece of paper or a telegram."

Rainer smiled. "Well, I love my cows, you know. I might get to jabbering away about them for hours at a time. Just tell me when you get bored."

Ada smiled and agreed. Rainer then began telling her about what he did on his farm, how he milked the cows, fixed the fences, and did anything else required of him. Ada was very interested in how he milked the cows.

"I actually have a boy who comes over and helps me with the milking," Rainer explained. "If you're interested in helping, I definitely need the hands."

"I'm not an expert milker," Ada laughed, "but I would be very interested in trying it out."

"Maybe after a few lessons, you'll find you are a natural."

Ada was disappointed to see them pulling into the drive in front of a log house. "This is my family's house," Rainer explained.

"Where do you live?" Ada asked.

Rainer put his arm around her and pointed to the West. "If you look, you might be able to distinguish my house against the moon's light."

Ada was more focused on how his arm felt around her shoulders. She tried to find the house, moving her face around. "I think I see it," Ada said, even though she wasn't sure.

"It's about another fifteen minutes from here by road, unless you get to galloping on a horse."

"Now horse riding is something I can do," Ada said. She was thankful for the horse riding lessons she had had when she was young.

"Let's go inside," Rainer said. He brought her into the house and introduced his mother and father. They were just laying out dinner, and Ada's stomach rumbled. That lunch she had not eaten meant she was empty and ready to eat.

Ada tried to be polite to everyone. "Let me get Ada's trunk," Rainer said. "I'll be back." He went outside and briefly left Ada by herself. She smiled at everyone nervously.

"It's nice to have you here," Rainer's mother- Rachel- said.

Ada nodded. "Thank you for being so accommodating. I know it must put you out to have a stranger among you."

Rainer's father, Benjamin, shook his head. "No, I much prefer it this way. It's better you stay here while you and Rainer get to know one another, before you get married and find out that your letters were poor representations of who you really are."

Ada was silent. She could tell that Rainer's father did not approve of their method of finding each other. She merely looked around and noted that the house was mostly quiet. There were no small children. Ada was under the impression that Western families always had a lot of children.

"Do you have any more children?" Ada asked politely.

Rachel nodded. "Yes, we have five children total. Three have married and moved out. Rainer just finished building his own house, and Ella is probably out there with our baby pigs. She is crazy about baby animals."

"How old is Ella?" Ada asked.

"Sixteen," Rachel replied. Ada nodded and looked around the house as she stood awkwardly in the doorway. "Come," Rachel said. "Sit down, and I will serve you a plate."

"Thank you," Ada said. "But perhaps I should wait for Rainer first."

She saw Rachel give Benjamin a look, but she could only guess what was passing between both of Rainer's parents. When Rainer finally came in with his sister in tow, they all sat down and ate dinner. Ada found Ella very friendly, even though she was five years younger than herself. Ada knew that she would get along well with Ella. Now, Ada only had to worry about how things would work out without Rainer.

"I am going to ride over to my house," Rainer said. He made eye contact with Ada. "Would you like to go outside with me for a few minutes?"

Ada nodded and tried to keep the smile off her face. She had been wanting a few minutes to speak privately with Rainer. They sat outside the cabin on two stools. The only light came from the fire inside that leaked light through the cracks.

"Would you really like to help with milking tomorrow?" Rainer asked.

"I would," Ada hesitated. "But my journey has tired me out. I think I may need to sleep late tomorrow. But perhaps the next day. . ."

Rainer nodded. "Of course. Don't worry. Another day will work just fine. How about after I finish everything that needs to be taken care of on the farm, I could drive you into town? If you are missing anything or you find that you need something, we can get it."

"I really don't need anything," Ada protested.

Rainer held up his hand. "Then I shall get you something you don't need. There is a woman in town who makes delicious ice cream. I'd like to get you a cone."

Ada smiled. She liked the idea. "Okay, I'll be ready then."

"Good night," Rainer said. He stood as did Ada. There was a moment of awkwardness as they tried to decide how to say goodbye. They finally both waved. Rainer mounted his horse and disappeared into the darkness. Ada sat outside for a few minutes by herself, thinking over her day. When she started nodding off, she realized she should go to bed before she fell off the stool and hurt herself.

Chapter 4

The next day, Ada waited anxiously for the time when Rainer would arrive. He did not disappoint, and he came over just in time for the midday meal. After they had eaten, he told her he would ready the carriage and take her for ice cream.

"Oh, can't I go?" Ella asked.

Rainer didn't even take a moment to think about his answer. "Of course. I can't keep my baby sister ice cream free."

"I'm not your baby sister."

"Oh, do I have another sister younger than you?" Rainer teased, pretending to look around. His voice dropped as though they were discussing an important, secret matter. "Is Ma going to have another child?"

Ella laughed. "I wish she would, but you know that won't happen. Let me go change into my nice shoes."

"You don't mind, do you?" Rainer asked, turning to Ada.

Ada shook her head, even though she did mind. She had wanted to experience this first outing alone with Rainer. She felt as though if she went out with brother and sister, she would immediately feel let out of all their jokes.

"Let's go," Rainer said. Ella hurried toward the carriage, but Rainer purposely boosted Ada first before helping his sister in. Ada felt her cheeks warm as Rainer pushed into the carriage and sat right next to her. She could feel his leg pressed against hers, and Ada swallowed a few times to keep her mouth from growing dry.

Rainer teased Ella about her money for ice cream, asking her how she planned to buy one when she didn't have any money. Ada smiled. These two were close, and that said something about Rainer. Ada knew there were seven years between the two, but she liked how close they were. She liked the jokester, generous side of him that she hadn't quite been able to grasp through his letters.

When they reached town, Rainer helped them both down. He walked in the middle and held his arm out. Ada looped her arm through Rainer's and smiled as they chatted. The more she talked to him, the more she felt as though this was the kind of man she could spend the rest of her life with.

They reached the ice cream parlor and stepped inside. The parlor only offered five different flavors and was very different from the pharmacy where Ada got her ice cream in New York. She looked at the flavors and knew immediately that she wanted chocolate. Nothing else appealed to her. Even though there were not a menagerie of flavors, Ella took perhaps ten minutes scanning the flavors.

"What are you getting, Ada?" she finally asked.

"Chocolate," Ada answered easily. "I love anything chocolate, and I probably indulged in it too much in my earlier days." Ada stopped herself before she went too deep into her memories.

"I think chocolate is a good idea," Ella said. "I'll have chocolate as well," Ella said. Rainer ordered their ice creams and handed each of the cones to them paired with a gallant bow.

They sat down at a small table and began eating their ice cream. Rainer and Ella began talking about some of the latest town news. Ada listened in.

"I'm sorry," Rainer said, in the middle of saying something to his sister. "We must have been boring you incredibly. I didn't mean to make conversation about something you wouldn't know, but. . ."

"Please," Ada said, smiling. "Don't worry yourself about it. I am finding it quite interesting learning about my new town."

"So," Ella broke in. "Are you two really going to marry just because you wrote letters to each other?"

Ada's cheeks turned red. This was one of those questions that made the person speechless when they received it, but later on, they knew exactly how they would answer. Ada slid a look at Rainer who was smiling at her. "I guess that's what we're going to find out, Ella. Maybe you should keep your nose in your own business."

Ella gave her brother an annoyed look. "I just wanted to know. It seems a little strange to me."

"You seem a little strange to me," Rainer replied, ducking from his sister's retaliation. Ada stood and threw her napkin in the bin.

Rainer copied suit and held out his arm for her to use once again. Ada slipped her hand into the crook of his elbow as Ella caught up with them. "Did you discover you needed anything?" Rainer asked.

"Um, no, I have everything," Ada said, feeling strange about Rainer's freedom to spend money on anything she might request.

"Surely you need something. Perhaps you and Ella can go together into the general store. I do need to buy some meat. My icebox is almost empty. I shall leave you two here and meet you back in half an hour. Surely you can find something to occupy your time during then," Rainer said.

The two women nodded and watched Rainer took off with a purposeful stride. "Where would you like to go?" Ella asked.

Ada shrugged. "You know this town much better than I do. I might simply like to walk for a bit." The two girls got to know each other as they took a walk through the town. Ada enjoyed meeting new people. Many seemed to know Ella, and they all asked who her new friend was.

Ada found herself the center of attention. "Has the time passed yet?" she asked Ella. Ella nodded.

"I believe it has. Let's go back. If we are late, my brother won't be happy."

The two made their way back to the corner, and Ada was not happy when she saw who was standing there waiting for them. Rainer was talking with Kaya. Ada set her jaw, wanting to hang back so that Rainer wouldn't notice them. Maybe if they hung back, then she could see how Rainer acted when he didn't anyone was watching him.

Kaya laid her hand on Rainer's arm as she laughed. Rainer was laughing too, and Ada's stomach felt sick. What did he find so funny about this woman? What were they talking about?

Ella burst forward to join the two. "Has it been half an hour already? I feel like the time just flies. Ava and I didn't think you would be here yet."

Rainer nodded. "Yes, but don't worry. I haven't minded the waiting."

Ava hung back. She was really hurt by the fact that the one time that she left Rainer alone, he would start talking with this woman and let her put her hands all over him. She had a right to act hurt, but if she acted hurt, then there was no way she would be able to get Rainer's attention again.

Ava stepped forward. "It's nice to see you again, Kaya," Ava said, resisting offering a curtsy.

Ella looked confused. "You know this woman. I've never seen her before. Are you new in town?" Ella asked Kaya.

Kaya nodded. "Yes, I just came in yesterday on the train." She answered as one would answer an annoying pet that kept barking at her.

"Oh, are you going to be staying in town for long?" Ada was glad that Ella had the courage to ask all the questions on Ada's mind.

"Yes," Kaya nodded. "I just moved here. My family lived her when I was little. I thought it would be a good place to find a husband."

Ava couldn't believe Kaya was so open about her intentions, and even more than that, Ava couldn't believe that Rainer was not disgusted by Kaya's obvious desperation.

"So, you'll be here for a while then?" Rainer asked.

"If all goes well, then I hope to live here for the rest of my life," Kaya said, smiling in a sickly sweet way at Rainer.

Ava made a face then quickly changed her expression to a neutral one. She couldn't have Rainer asking her about why she was so resistant to this woman. Some men simply didn't understand. But then, Ava couldn't believe her ears.

"I'm sure my Ma wouldn't mind if I invited you for dinner sometime. I'll warn her, but I am fairly sure that any evening would be fine. She would hate for a new woman in town to be eating by herself every night."

Kaya smiled. "Of course," she smiled. "Thank you for your invitation. I shall be sure to accept your invitation one evening this week. It's not easy moving back to a town from your childhood. It seems as though most people don't remember me. They know of my parents, but that doesn't make it any easier for me."

Ava watched as Kaya successfully secured it. "I'm sure that is hard," Rainer agreed. "I can't imagine living somewhere far away from my family."

"Well," Rainer said, glancing at his watch. "The meat is going to get warm. We should probably go. I shall talk to you later." Ella and Ava said goodbye as well. As Ava was helped into the carriage this time, she didn't feel as happy as she had when they set out that morning.

Chapter 5

Ava spent the next three days exploring Rainer's farm. "I wasn't sure what I thought about a cattle farm," Ada said.

"Why?" Rainer said, giving her an odd look as though it was strange anyone could have a problem with cows.

"Because," Ada said. She smiled, because she knew how Rainer would react. "I've never seen a cow before."

"What?" Rainer's surprise soon gave way to laughter. "Don't they herd cattle where you live? There have to be fields close to the city."

Ada shook her head. "No. My landlady would buy fresh milk every morning, but the man who sold it didn't bring the cow along with him."

Rainer laughed. "I wouldn't bring my cows along either. I use them mostly for breeding, but when they don't have a baby, why wouldn't I take the milk?"

"Do you sell it?" Ada asked. "I haven't seen you coming down the streets making sales."

"I take it to the general store every morning. Mr. Baines buys it from me and sells it to his customers. I keep some of it to make butter. Do you know how to churn butter?"

Ada shook her head. "No, show me how."

Rainer laughed again. "I don't know how. I know the basic process. It includes a lot of movement, but I don't know the specific techniques. My ma can help you out in that area."

Rainer put his hand on his stomach. "I think my stomach is telling me it is supper time. Are you hungry?"

Ada nodded. She wanted to eat a private dinner with Rainer, but he always ate dinner at his ma's house. Ada wasn't quite sure why he had moved over there if he was going to spend some much time there.

They paused in the doorway of his house, and Ada looked around. As soon as she had first seen the house, she began imagining how she could put some touches of home in it. Ada turned back. Rainer was right behind her, and Ada smiled gently.

"When we live here," she ventured to say. "I will make you a special dinner every night."

"You will, will you?" Rainer asked, his thumb coming up and gently stroking her jaw. The touch made Ada feel nervous. She knew that she felt strongly for Rainer, but she had been unsure of his feelings until that very moment. "I think I'll enjoy that very much, a special dinner for the two of us."

"What do you like to eat?" Ada said, taking Rainer's rough hand between her own. She didn't want to go yet. She didn't want to walk across those fields and enter his mom's house, missing this romantic moment.

"My favorite? Oh, I love some good mashed potatoes with some homemade butter. That's my favorite." He looked down at her, and Ada suddenly realized how close they were standing. "But anything you cook, I would be happy to try."

Ada felt her breath come quickly. She looked down at Rainer's lips and back into his eyes. A smile twitched on his lips. He gently bent down and kissed her lips. Ada leaned into his lips and felt them softly part. When Rainer pulled back, his face was completely serious. But the moment Ada smiled, Rainer's face popped into a smile too.

Ada wanted to say something. She wanted to tell Rainer that his kiss had been everything she wanted it to be. She wanted to ask him when they were going to get married. She had come out here to be his bride, but Rainer seemed content to wait.

"Come on," Rainer said. "My ma will begin to wonder where we are."

Ada nodded and took Rainer's extended hand. They walked hand in hand the distance to his ma's house. It took them twenty minutes, and it took every ounce of Ada's strength not to jabber his ear off. She wanted to keep the silence and replay the moment in her head. Just a few minutes before they entered Rachel and Benjamin's cabin, Ada smiled at Rainer. He smiled at her, and Ada knew they shared a special secret.

When Ada stepped inside and saw Kaya seated comfortably at the table, Ada felt her stomach drop. Rainer let go of Ada's hand and went over to greet Kaya. Ada was cordial, but she could not bring herself to be friendly. Even though she was scolding her own behavior, Ada could not help but be jealous. Rainer seemed to be so friendly with Kaya, and he barely knew her.

"I am so glad you were able to find your way here," Rainer said. Kaya smiled back. She spotted Ada in the doorway and seemed confused, but she continued right on with her conversation with Rainer, not caring how Ada felt. Wasn't Ada going to marry Rainer? Hadn't he said as much? Why would he act so different now?

Ada swallowed as she realized that he hadn't mentioned it since in their letters. Maybe the only reason he hadn't married her yet was that he was distracted by Kaya. Maybe *that* was the whole reason it was taking them so long to "get to know each other."

Ada settled on the corner of the couch, wanting to know everything that passed between Kaya and Rainer, yet not wanting to hear how amiable Rainer sounded the whole time. Ada started worrying about what would happen should Rainer decide not to marry her. Ada felt as if she was choking in the heat of the fire. Ada stood and walked over to the doorway where the cool air was coming in. She couldn't go back to New York. She had already been shunned by her family, what was left of it.

Ada swallowed over and over, licking her lips and trying to make herself feel normal. Would she have to stay in Topeka and watch Rainer and Kaya have children together? Ada stepped outside to brush away the two tears that rushed out without permission.

"God," Ada said quietly. "Please, please." She didn't know what else to say as she begged God for mercy on her situation. "I can't go back, but I wouldn't have the money to stay here. I used up almost everything staying with the landlord in New York. Please have mercy. I thought this was what you wanted for me."

Ada was silent and felt a gentle breeze that seemed to come straight from heaven to her. It helped her feel peaceful. It was as though that wind carried the words "Trust Me."

"I'm trying," Ada protested, then she realized she wasn't really trying at all. She had just assumed that everything was going wrong, so she began to let her fears take over. "God, help me trust you," Ada said. She took a deep breath and was just about to step inside when she saw Rainer standing in the doorway.

"Is everything alright, Ada?" he asked.

Ada nodded, trying to force a smile for him. Rainer's smile was not forced by any means. "Come on," he said. "My ma has dinner ready, and she doesn't want it to get cold. You're hungry, aren't you?"

Ada nodded as Rainer took her hand and led her in to a spot on the bench beside himself. Ella and Kaya sat across from them. They all held hands to bless the meal, then Ada began eating. Rainer amiably made conversation with them all. Every time he turned and looked at Ada, she felt warmth in her stomach.

Chapter 6

Ada was disappointed when Rainer offered to drive Kaya back into town. She said that she had asked someone to drive her out there, but she did not have a way back. It was the perfect excuse, of course, but Ada was still disappointed. She did not like the idea of Rainer being with Kaya alone.

Ada dejectedly changed into her nightdress and combed out her hair. She was sharing a bed with Ella, and Ella was getting ready for bed as well.

"If I didn't know that my brother had sent for you to marry him, I would think he was quite taken with that Kaya."

Ella's words were not the ones Ada wanted to hear. Ada nodded, not being able to add her thoughts without crying.

Ella turned and saw Ada's serious face. "Don't worry. My brother's just always friendly to everyone." She seemed to be saying the exact opposite of what she had said only a moment earlier.

"I prefer not to talk about it," Ada said. "I'm very tired, and I need to get up for milking tomorrow." With that, Ada lay down on the bed and shut her eyes, pretending to be asleep.

The next morning, Ada showed up early for the milking. She tied an apron around her waist and made her way out to the barn. By now, she was comfortable around the cows. While she still was scared that one of them would step on her, she didn't shy away from the smell anymore.

"Good morning!" Rainer said, stepping out of the barn.

"Oh, am I late?" Ada asked, her eyes dropping to the ground.

Rainer shook his head. "You're right on time." He came forward and took one of her hands. "Come on, let's get this milking done, so I can let them out to pasture."

Ada sat down on the stool that was set up in her milking stall. Across the aisle, Rainer was milking another cow. His more experienced hands finished three cows in the time it took her to do one, but Ada was learning. She worked out her stress as she finished milking the cow. She needed to talk with Rainer about Kaya. She had to know how Rainer felt. If he felt something for Kaya, she would need another plan, because she couldn't stay in that town either. With about five cows left, Rainer suggested she go inside and make breakfast while he finished up and let them all out to pasture.

Ada quickly whipped up some eggs. She got out the bread she had made the day before and spread some jam on it. She placed the food on the table and waited for Rainer to come in.

"Let's pray," Rainer said. He bowed his head and thanked God for the food then began digging in.

"Rainer," Ada said softly. He looked up. "You know, I've been here more than a week, and we still haven't talked of getting married. I came out here to be your bride, didn't I?"

Rainer smiled at her. "Getting impatient, are you?"

"No," Ada immediately protested. "I just, I'm confused, what with your behavior toward Kaya, and no mention of a marriage."

"Surely you didn't think I wasn't going to marry you," Rainer protested. Ada shrugged. She felt silly admitting it now. Rainer stood and left his breakfast at the table as he pulled her to her feet. He forced her to look into his eyes. "I don't want you to be confused anymore," Rainer said. "Yes, I am going to marry you. I would never bring you away from your hometown, your family, everything, unless my intentions were true."

Ada swallowed, her secret weighing heavily on her. Could Rainer really love her if he didn't know the truth about everything that she had done before she came to Topeka? A part of her whispered that the past was in the past; all had been forgiven. But another part of her was nervous. She was worried Rainer would eventually find out and never trust her again.

Ada pulled Rainer into a hug and laid her head on his chest. She could feel his heart beating. Rainer wrapped his arms around her and gently kissed the top of her head.

"Ada," Rainer said gently. "I will marry you today if that is what you want."

Ada's heart almost felt like it was going to stop beating right then. She couldn't. He had to know, No, he didn't. Ada went back and forth in her mind, and Rainer pulled back from her, easing her chin up as he watched the emotions pass over her face.

"Something's wrong," he said, shaking his head.

This was all wrong! Why hadn't she just agreed as soon as he said it?

"Do you find yourself unhappy here?" Rainer asked, lifting his eyebrows.

Ada shook her head hurriedly. "No, I love your family, and I lo-" Ada broke off. "I enjoy getting to know you. I couldn't imagine my future in any other city with any other family."

"Then, what's the trouble?" Rainer asked.

Ada took a deep breath. She felt the unasked for tears rising to the surface. She was ruining everything! Rainer took another step backward as though her tears were scaring him. He shook his head. Ada wanted to reach out and grab him, force him to hug her again as he had been doing, force him to love her and ignore her secrets.

"I'm sorry," Ada said, quickly wiping her fingers under her eyes. "We should eat up the breakfast before it gets cold."

Rainer sat down at the table and began eating, but Ada found that she could not eat. She stirred the food around on her plate then asked Rainer if he would like some more. He shook his head. "Look," he said. "I know it must be hard being away from your family. If this isn't right for you, you should decide that now before we get married."

Ada's stomach clenched up. She couldn't imagine feeling as strongly about a man as she felt about Rainer, but he seemed to be distancing himself from her. Ada knew that if she wanted to hold onto this man, she would have to tell him everything.

Chapter 7

"Rainer," Ada said, following him to the door. "I need to talk to you."

Rainer turned around and studied her. "What's wrong?" he asked.

Ada wanted to take his hand and pull him back to the kitchen table. She didn't want to have this conversation while he was standing in the doorway, glancing out to the barn, and thinking about his chores. At the same time, she didn't have the courage to be bold and bring him back to the table.

"I am responsible for my sister's death," Ada said.

Rainer raised his eyebrows then did exactly what Ada had been wanting. He guided her back to the kitchen table, and they sat facing each other. "What happened?" Rainer asked.

Ada tried to swallow back the tears, but they seemed insistent on coming anyway. The tears spilled over, and Ada sobbed as she told her story. "It happened about three months ago. The weather was warm, and my mom asked me to watch my younger sister. Penelope was her name." Ada swallowed slowly as Rainer put his hand on top of hers.

"I decided to take her swimming. We stopped by my friend's house. I asked her if she wanted to come. She came with us. Penelope was three years old. When we got to the pond, there were plenty of children who had the same idea. I shooed Penelope into the water, preferring to talk with my friend instead of watching her. I heard children's shouts and saw Penelope in the middle of the pond. She went under the water. I know now, it must have been the tenth or twelfth time she went under. She was drowning. I stood watching her. I wasn't able to move. I counted the seconds, waiting for her to come up. She never did. I finally swam out and found her. . .her body. She was dead."

Ada was crying, and she lost her ability to talk. She laid her face on her hands and sobbed. How could she have been so thoughtless? If she had just looked at her sister instead of her friend, if she had been more careful, or moved more quickly, she could have saved her. Rainer wrapped his arms around her, but it didn't make Ada feel any better.

When her sobs had finished wracking through her body, Ada looked up and wiped her face. "My parents told me I was not welcome in their house any longer. I had to move out. I wanted to come here to escape. I enjoyed talking with you through our letters, but," Ada swallowed, wanting to tell the truth completely. "Honestly, I did not care who the man was, as long as I could get away from my hometown and start over. I didn't like the people looking at me and whispering. I wanted to be normal, accepted, and loved."

Rainer gently rubbed the top of her hand. He didn't look angry or condemning. He looked like he might understand her. "Ada," he said, causing her to look into his eyes, urgently hoping he would be able to forgive her.

"I would never hold such a mistake against you," he said. "What happened was an accident, not something you purposely did."

Ada furrowed her brows.

"I'm sure you loved Penelope, am I right?"

"I never showed her how much I loved her," Ada said, her voice full of regret. She suddenly gave a sob that had a smile. "I remember how she would get home from going out with either me or my mother, and she would throw her shoes into the air and begin running around the house. She hated shoes."

Rainer smiled. "They can be quite cumbersome for a little child."

"I just," Ada was back to thinking on her current situation. "I want to start over. I didn't want you to know. I felt like you might decide I wasn't ready. But, since I came here, I realized that I don't only like the idea of leaving my town, I really like you."

Rainer kissed her forehead. "You know what, Ada? I like you as well. In fact, I really want to marry you."

"Marry me," Ada repeated the words like a child fascinated with the idea. "Yes, please," Ada said.

Rainer stood and took both of her hands. He pulled her closer and kissed her lips with such promise that Ada was left breathless.

"Yes," Rainer said. "I'll marry you. You can be my wife, and I will be your husband. We can have a family together."

Ada smiled widely. "Yes," she said. She hugged Rainer tightly. She wanted to shout. She felt so filled with joy. "We will get married and have a life together."

"Forever and ever," Rainer whispered gently. "Ada, would you have time in your busy day today to go to the courthouse?"

Ada's stomach dropped as she nodded. This was really happening. She was going to marry this man. "I think I can perhaps make time for you," she teased, her fears relived from having told him her darkest secret.

"Do you have something special to wear?" Rainer asked.

Ada nodded. "Yes, I have a special white dress that I sewed myself."

Rainer smiled. "Tell my Ma and Pa to drive you into town. I will meet you at the courthouse at ten o'clock."

Ada wrapped her arms around Rainer and smiled again, delirious with joy. "I shall tell them right now." She took a few running steps toward his parents' cabin before she turned back. "I forgot something." Rainer looked confused for a moment, but then Ada kissed him, her soft lips pressed against his. She pulled back, and he was smiling widely at her.

"I'm going to marry you," Ada said.

Rainer nodded. "Yes, you are. Now, go. Go get ready!"

THE BABY BUGGY

Chapter One

"Alright, Kip. Time to go into your stable," Aaron said to his horse as he gently tugged at its reins. Aaron walked besides Kip quietly but quick in pace as the sky above was becoming dark with rain clouds. He could already smell the scent of rain in the air; a scent he was all too enamored with. It reminded him of the day he and his wife, Sarah, were married over seven years ago, in the middle of a thunderstorm. The claps of thunder during their Amish wedding ceremony were so loud that at times, they were unable to hear the words spoken by the bishop. For over seven years, Aaron and Sarah had attempted to conceive a child. Sadly, with no success—until now. Many months they waited to see the results of their work but Sarah's cycle never ceased; the dreaded cycle that filled them both with feelings of incompetence and disappointment. The fact that their friends got pregnant on the first time sometimes gave them a tiny bit of envy, although, they were always happy for anybody who was able to enjoy such a blessing. A few weeks ago, Sarah's dreaded cycle did not reset and her monthly visitor missed its appearance. When this occurred, their mind did not automatically think about the cause being a pregnancy. Although they had always remained hopeful, it simply did not seem possible. They were convinced that their last attempt had been successful when Sarah, who was always healthy as a horse, became extremely ill. A pelvic exam performed by their Amish settlement's midwife confirmed that Sarah was indeed with child.

As Aaron removed the bridle from Kip's head he thought about how life would change once their child was born and was filled with gratefulness. All of those years of pain from being unable to procreate vanished the moment they found out about their baby. Aaron was definitely excited about what the future held for him and his growing family. He picked up a brush from a pail and brushed Kip's mane. When he was finished, he draped a green blanket over the horse's back. Then, he quickly made his way back inside the farmhouse expecting

Sarah to greet him so lovingly as she usually did. As soon as Aaron shut the door behind him the rumbling started from the skies. The fire was going in the fireplace but Sarah was nowhere to be seen or heard.

"Sarah?" Aaron called out to the silent house. He went to the kitchen thinking Sarah was still preparing dinner but she was not there. He called out again. The house stood eerily quiet, something was wrong—he knew it. He slowly started to make his way around their home, opening doors expecting to find Sarah. He called out to Sarah, this time more frantically. It was highly unusual for Sarah to not be home at this time. Finally, he stepped into their bedroom which was located towards the very back of the house. The bathroom door was slightly opened and he could see dim candlelight. Aaron pushed the door open to find Sarah sitting with her head in her hands on the bathroom floor in her nightgown. She was crying.

"Sarah, what's wrong?" Aaron asked her bending down next to her. Then, he saw. Sarah was sitting in a pool of her own blood.

"Oh, god, Sarah. What happened? Did you hurt yourself?"

"Something is wrong with the baby. All of a sudden I just started bleeding profusely," Sarah said through sobs. Aaron put his hands on her face and realized that she was soaked in sweat.

"You're burning up. We have to get you to the midwife right this instant," Aaron said as he tried to help her up. Sarah let out a bloodcurdling cry.

"Okay, okay," Aaron said, "I'll be back, Sarah. Don't move. I'm going to bring the midwife. Please, stay here." Aaron bolted out the house in the pouring rain. He arrived at the midwife's house and pounded on the door. A man, the midwife's husband, opened the door with a bothered look on his face.

"Why are you knocking like so?" the man asked, "We are in the middle of dinner and you come knocking like a madman. What do you want?"

"I'm so sorry, Jett. Bertha must come quickly, something is very wrong with Sarah and the baby," Aaron told him catching his breath. At that moment, Bertha, the midwife, came to the door.

"What's going on with Sarah?" She asked worriedly.

"She's bleeding and in pain. Please, Bertha. Come quick!"

By the time Aaron and Bertha made it to the house, they can hear Sarah's screams coming from inside. They carried Sarah to the bed and laid her down. Bertha sent Aaron to the kitchen to gather supplies for her examination.

"Sarah, I think you are in labor," Bertha told Sarah.

"No, this can't be happening. This baby is not due for another twenty weeks or so," Sarah cried.

"Aaron, I think you better get to a phone to call for an ambulance. It seems like she's hemorrhaging and you know our supplies are limited here at the settlement. If we want her to be safe, we have to get her to a hospital quickly." The events following Sarah's predicament were a blur to Aaron. He remembered the hospital and the doctor telling him about his child's death. He felt a sense of relief when the doctor told him Sarah was recovering and that she would be well physically, but was hit with pain like from a gunshot wound when they also explained that Sarah had an emergency hysterectomy. If their chances of having a baby were little before, their chances would definitely be impossible for the rest of their lives. The rest of that night and even the following days were blurry and muffled. Aaron didn't recall doing anything but sit next to his brokenhearted wife's bed.

Chapter Two

A year had passed since the loss of their unborn child and of any hope they had of growing their family with children of their own. Other members of their Amish settlement would sometimes ask why they didn't consider adoption. Truthfully, they had but it was much too expensive and did not have that amount of money. For the most part, people did not mention the loss to them. It seemed to have been forgotten by the other members but never by Aaron and Sarah. On the anniversary of the unborn child's death, they went out into the fields to pick flowers. They were making an arrangement of yellow, purple and red wildflowers.

"We should start heading back soon," Sarah said looking up at the sky, "it seems that rain clouds are rolling in."

"You're right. Let's just cut a couple more and we can get going," Aaron replied.

"How fitting, right?" Sarah asked him. He was kneeling cutting stems and her question made him freeze. He turned to look at her. Sarah was looking at the bunch of flowers she cradled in her arms.

"I'm not going to cry," she said.

"You should, if you feel like it," Aaron told her placing his hands on her shoulders.

"No, that won't bring our baby back now, will it?"

"It won't but we should not keep our emotions all pent up." Sarah walked over to Kip and began loading the flowers they had collected into the buggy. Aaron followed behind her and before helping her up onto her seat he wrapped his arms around her.

"You're the strongest person I know," he told her, "I'm so glad that *you're* still here. You were part of our child and you're still here. I'll always have our baby with me as long as you're living with me, too."

"That's beautiful. What a nice way of putting it, Aaron. Thank you," Sarah replied with a smile. They finished loading up their buggy and soon, they were on their way back home.

That night Sarah baked some decadent desserts in celebration of their baby's short life. The baby had died but it had also lived and was very loved in that time span. In order to lift their spirits, they also played a few board and card games. It was obvious in the way that the couple interacted and spent the time in each other's presence that after all they had gone through, they were very much in love. After their fun-filled night, they joined in bed and said their good nights.

The thunder had begun and the rain was starting to land heavily on their rooftop. A few hours after they had gone to sleep, they heard a loud crash; anybody could have confused it with the wind causing an object to fall or with thunder. Aaron laid in bed listening to the sounds coming from outside when he heard a neigh.

"We secured Kip's stable right?" Sarah asked still half-asleep.

"I'm sure we did." Aaron said as he got up to find his coat. There was another clash outside. He thought that maybe the thunder had spooked Kip and he tried to come looking for them.

"If you're sure, why are you going outside in the rain?" Sarah asked in the dark.

"Just for sanity's sake!" He replied shutting the room door behind him.

Once he got outside he realized the horse that neighed was not Kip. There was a black horse with a buggy tied to it standing by Kip's stable. The buggy was damaged and Aaron could tell that the horse had run right through the fence from the picket still stuck in the wood. Aaron ran to the horse to see if people had been hurt in the buggy. The horse trotted away from him in fright. He let Kip out of the stable to see if it would calm the other horse down. Kip followed the horse and eventually, the horse allowed Aaron to get close enough. From the outside, there didn't appear to be anybody in the buggy. Aaron figured that maybe someone had left their horse outside during the storm and the horse took off in search for shelter from the thunder. He walked up to the horse and stroked its wet face telling it that it would be okay. He walked behind the buggy and opened up the small white curtain. At first glance, it appeared empty but in the darkness he could make out a bundled up yellow blanket. He reached for it and he froze when he felt a soft body, still warm. He gently picked it up with two hands and pulled it closer to himself for inspection. He moved the blanket a little to see who or what was wrapped in it. Aaron stood there looking into the face of a baby not older than a few weeks. He immediately went into protector mode; wrapping the baby to shield it from the rain and ran as fast as his legs could go back into the house where Sarah was waiting for him in the living room. Sarah walked over to Aaron when she saw how concerned he had returned. Her initial thought was that Kip actually had escaped his stable and had run off or gotten injured but then she saw the bundle he was carrying.

"What's this?" Sarah asked but she could already tell that it was a baby from its shape.

"A horse came crashing through the community fence looking for shelter. This baby was in the buggy but nobody else was around," he answered breathlessly. Once Sarah realized that this baby could be critically hurt she gently picked it up from Aaron's arms.

"It's warm so that must mean it is alive," Sarah said examining the baby's face. She gently laid it on the couch and unwrapped the yellow blanket. The baby was wearing a white silky nightgown. Sarah undressed the baby and examined the limbs one-by-one. At the same time, she was in awe of the smoothness of the baby's skin and its ability to sleep through all of the commotion.

"It smells a little—odd," Aaron said with his nose in the air.

"We should change the baby to prevent a rash. Please bring me some cloth and pins," Sarah instructed her husband. Slowly the baby began to rustle awake and it was at this time that Sarah began to feel nervous. She was afraid the baby would not like them or want its parents and make a big fuss for their neighbors to hear.

"I'm going back to the buggy," Aaron told Sarah as he returned with the cloth and pins.

"What for?" Sarah asked.

"Well, people are going to ask questions when they find that a foreign horse and an empty buggy appeared in our fields. I also want to see if whoever had this baby left behind any baby supplies in there. The baby will wake soon and it will be hungry."

"You have a good point," Sarah said as she slowly removed the baby's diaper. It was in that moment when they discovered the baby was a girl.

"Oh, Aaron. It's a beautiful baby girl," Sarah said happily.

"Yes, she is quite beautiful," Aaron replied as he put his coat back on. Kip and the strange horse had walked back to the stable by that time. It was still raining pretty heavily so Aaron quickly untied the horse from the buggy and put it in the stable next to Kip. There was not much room for two horses but they would only be in there for one night since Aaron planned on finding the owners the next morning. Aaron dried off the horse with a towel before searching the buggy.

Inside of the buggy, Aaron found shopping bags with food and supplies. Thankfully, among the groceries was a small tin of powder formula for the baby. He hadn't spotted the bags during his initial search because the baby had diverted his attention. Aaron also found a small purple coin purse in one of the shopping bags. Upon opening the purse, he found no money but he did find a photo less identification card belonging to a woman, presumably the baby's mother or guardian. Aaron had so many questions about the entire situation. Where are the baby's parents? Why was the horse so startled? Why did the parents leave behind their baby and groceries in a buggy? Answers were going to have to wait. The only thing that mattered was that the baby was well taken care of and safely returned to her parent's arms. Aaron put the groceries back in the bag and left them there but he took the baby formula with him. When Aaron entered the house again a few minutes later, Sarah was still on the couch with the baby girl. She had already changed her diaper and had wrapped her in a fresh blanket.

"I found formula," Aaron said holding up the tin.

"Oh, good!" Sarah exclaimed.

"We might have a small problem, however," Aaron continued, "We don't have any bottles to put her formula in." Sarah told him otherwise. After their baby had died, they put away all of his belongings and kept them in their bedroom closet. It was not many things; a bottle, a few blankets and onesies. That was all that was left of that time in their lives when they were parents and Sarah could not bring herself to give away those belongings. Following the directions on the tin of formula, Aaron made the baby's bottle.

"Alright, here we go," he said handing the bottle to Sarah who was cradling the baby ever so affectionately. She put the nipple to the baby's lip and surprisingly, she took it right away. Sarah cooed at the baby as she watched her eat and make the cutest sounds.

"We should go to bed now. It's really late and we have to wake in the morning to ask around the community for the parents of this baby," Aaron told Sarah while he stroked the baby girl's head. They made their way back to the bedroom and put the sleeping baby on their bed.

"You can sleep on the bed with the baby," Aaron told her, "I'll sleep on the couch so I can hear if anybody comes looking for her." He walked over to the bed and sat down. He watched as Sarah caressed the baby's rosy cheeks and ginger hair. She traced the baby's palms with her finger and whispered sweet things to her trying to comfort her even though the baby was nowhere near distressed.

"What should we call her?" Sarah finally asked.

"Well, I think we should wait for her parents to come find her and we can ask for her name then."

"What if they don't come?"

"They will. Who would abandon their child this way? We wouldn't, would we? It wouldn't make sense."

"I hope they can leave her with us," Sarah told him.

"Sarah, that's a horrible thing to say. This baby needs her real parents. I hope they come as soon as possible; I'm sure they are missing her miserably."

"I guess," Sarah sighed. Aaron had already taken notice of Sarah's interactions with the baby. Sarah was already beginning to make the baby her own without even considering that the baby's parents could have showed up right then and there. However, it could not be helped—after all, Sarah never got to hold her own baby. Aaron refrained from saying anything else about the situation and left her to cuddle the baby in peace.

Chapter Three

Aaron was in a deep slumber when he was suddenly startled awake by a loud knocking on the door. He could tell from the dim light coming through the curtains that it was still a very cloudy morning. He opened the door to find two men and a woman standing on the porch.

"Yes, how can I help you?" He asked groggily.

"Good morning. We've come to ask about this run-down buggy by your stable. We heard a commotion last night and were wondering if that's the reason why," one of the older men said to him. Aaron went on to explain about the events of the night but for some reason, left out the details of finding a baby inside of the buggy. The woman began to whisper to the other man standing beside her.

"Is something else the matter?" Aaron asked curiously.

"We think this buggy might belong to an Amish couple from another community who were found murdered on the side of the road a few hours ago." Aaron was in complete disbelief.

"What else do you know?" Aaron asked them hoping they could give more information about the events of last night.

"That's pretty much it. They are not from our community or from the community a few miles away. We don't know much about them," the woman revealed.

"Are the police involved?"

"Yes, they are and they said the couple's baby is missing, too." Aaron tried his best to not look suspicious.

"Oh, wow. That's terrible," he told the people.

"Yes, it truly is. We must pray for this couple, whoever they are, and for their baby to be safe wherever it may be."

"Yes, we shall pray. Thank you for letting me know about the buggy. I am going to get in touch with the police as soon as I get dressed," Aaron said shutting the door.

"Well, if *that's* not suspicious," Sarah told Aaron. She was standing in the hallway as he spoke with the neighbors and she had heard everything. The baby was sound asleep bundled in her arms.

"What?" He asked.

"You basically shut the door in their face," she scolded.

"What would you have rather me do? Bring the baby to the door? I should have done that. This baby is not ours. Why are we hiding her?"

"We can't give her back. Her parents are dead, you heard. She needs loving parents. We can be that for her."

"We don't know if she has other family. What if she has siblings or grandparents? We can't rob them of her that way. I think this is kidnapping, Sarah."

"It is not kidnapping! She's a blessing. Don't you see, Aaron? Why would she appear on the anniversary of our child's death? God has surely sent her to us."

"God did not have her parents killed like animals out by the road to give us a baby. Please, be rational."

"We did not kidnap her. You found her. Why has nobody come looking for her?"

"I don't know. If her family comes looking for her, we *will* give her back."

"But she needs parents—,"

"Enough!" Aaron interrupted, "We are not liars and we do not keep things that are not ours. We are returning the baby and that's final."

"I'm not going to let this baby live without her mother. I'm her mother now!" Sarah exclaimed as she stomped back into the bedroom. Aaron could hear her crying from where he stood in the living room. He didn't know what to do. He felt as if taking the baby girl from Sarah would be like their baby dying all over again. He left her alone for the rest of the morning while he prepared himself to call the police over to return the horse and buggy. Aaron wanted to find out if the police knew who the couple was and if they had any family. He knew that the longer that Sarah was with the baby, the more they would bond and the harder it would be to return her to her family. Even though, regardless of when they returned her, Sarah would still be devastated.

Aaron phoned the police and let them know that the horse and buggy belonging to the couple had ended up in their Amish community in the middle of the night. The department sent the detective in charge of the homicide case along with forensic analysts. He went outside to meet with the detective, a short bald man, and told him what had occurred.

"There was nobody here with the horse?" The detective asked Aaron, looking him right in the eyes.

"No, sir. I did not see or hear any person around here. I just heard the horse crashing through the fence. When I came out, there was nobody around."

"Did you touch the buggy?"

"Yes, sir. I searched it to see if I could find who it belonged to. I did happen to find a coin purse with an identification card but I left it where I found it."

"Okay, well we are going to be a while here on your yard while we collect any evidence left behind by the perpetrator," the detective told him.

"Yes, yes. Take all the time you need. Detective, I heard that the couple also had a baby with them the last time that they were seen," Aaron said.

"The last people to see the couple alive were the owners of a convenience store not too far from here and they said they had a newborn with them but we have not found any baby."

"I see," Aaron said, "if you do find this couple's family—would it be possible for you to give me their contact information?"

"What for?" the detective asked.

"Oh, you know," Aaron answered, "we would like to pray with them and offer them any help or anything else they might need."

"That's very kind. We'll let you guys know once we find the community they were from."

"Okay, Detective. I will be working in the field just right over there. If you need anything else from me, please let me know." The men said their goodbyes and Aaron went straight to the field start on his daily tasks. He almost went to warn Sarah to stay inside the house and hide the baby but he knew Sarah would be more than just careful in order to keep the baby longer. He was quite distracted throughout the day, however, fearing that someone from the community would come inform him of the police taking his wife away for holding a baby hostage.

Aaron returned home after his work day right before sunset. He could smell the aroma of the warm dinner Sarah had prepared before he even entered his home. He found Sarah in the room with a freshly bathed baby. The baby was wide awake looking around the room. Every time that Sarah spoke to her, she cooed in reply. The dampness of her skin and freshness of the air made her cheeks and nose rosy. Sarah quickly wrapped the baby in her long sleeping gown to keep her warm. Her curls became wild after they air dried from the bath, giving her a rather comical look. Aaron looked at the baby's big gray eyes and unruly hair—he couldn't help but to laugh. Sarah and the baby both turned to look at him.

"I'm sorry," Aaron said trying to calm down, "She looks so funny."

"She does, doesn't she?" Sarah cracked a smile, "She sure is the cutest baby I've ever seen." Aaron could see the infatuation in his wife's eyes; the way she held the baby and cared for her revealed a tenderness she had been wanting to express to their own baby. Aaron had no doubt that Sarah would have been the most loving mother of them all. The baby was beginning to get drowsy and a bit fussy from hunger.

"I'll go make a bottle," Sarah told Aaron, "Do you mind holding onto her?" Aaron nodded his head.

"Wait, it's been years since I've held a baby. Maybe it's not a good idea," he told Sarah. It was true that he had not held a baby in a long time and that made him nervous. However, he was more afraid of falling in love with the baby girl that he knew they could not keep. He was afraid that holding a baby momentarily would bring back all those bitter thoughts and emotions about never being able to hold a child of his own.

"Don't be a scaredy cat," Sarah teased. She showed Aaron how to make his arms comfortable to cradle the baby and gently laid the baby on him. While Sarah was in the kitchen preparing the baby's meal, Aaron stared at the baby's features. He wondered what his child would have looked like full-term. Would it look like him or like Sarah? Would their baby have had curly hair like Sarah or straight like his? He gave his index finger to the baby and she gripped it tightly.

"Whoa, you're a strong little lady aren't you?" He said to her.

"Do you want to feed her?" Sarah said handing him the warm bottle. Aaron looked at Sarah unsure about what to say. He wanted to repeat to her that they had to find the baby's family but a part of him loved being in that moment with both of them finally taking care of a precious human being—theirs or not. The baby eagerly drank her formula and in the process, fell asleep. They laid her down on the bed and quietly exited the bedroom to have dinner themselves.

The two sat at the dinner table quietly—wanting to express themselves yet not wanting to fight. They both wanted a baby but Aaron never imagined it would happen like it did. He did not want either of them to get into trouble with the law for keeping the baby.

"I had so much fun with the baby today," Sarah started, "I think we might have to make a formula run to the store tomorrow morning.

I never knew a human so small could eat so much. She smiled at me a couple of times today; I almost melted." Aaron felt sad about how smitten Sarah was with a child who was not hers. Despite Sarah's stubbornness in regards to the situation, Aaron felt it was his responsibility to speak some logic to her.

"I think tomorrow we should go to the police and tell them we found the baby," Aaron told her. He didn't want her to be angry with him but he knew it was inevitable now.

"But they'll take her," Sarah says.

"She's not ours. We have to do things the right way, Sarah. God's way. I don't think he would approve of us hiding the baby this way."

"God sent this baby to us. I know he did. He wants to help me heal from the loss of our baby by having me be the mother of this beautiful baby girl."

"No. Our child died. That must mean that we are just not meant to be parents. It was not in God's plan for us."

"How can you say something like that? Are you saying that I would not make a good mother? Why do women who abandon their children get to bear them and not I? Because I'm not good enough?"

"You know that is not what I mean. Do you really want to rob her of a family? What will we tell her when she asks when she's older? You have to think about the future, too."

"Her parents are dead. God chose us to care for her. She could end up in foster care of be adopted by horrible people. Don't squander this blessing. I just know we won't ever get a chance like this ever again," Sarah said as her eyes began to cry. Aaron grabbed her hands and held them up to his face.

"I know you are still hurting, my love. I also lost a child last year, too. But this is not the right way to do things. We have kept her by lying. Do you plan on hiding her for the rest of her life? You hide her because you know we are not supposed to have her. Please, I am trying to protect us." Sarah sobbed quietly, not wanting to wake the baby. She knew her husband was only trying to do the right thing.

"If she is meant to be ours, God will show us the right path," Aaron assured her.

Chapter Four

After dinner, they went to bed and laid alongside the baby. Sarah let the tears silently roll down her face as she lamented having to say goodbye to the baby. They both caressed her tiny head and velvety cheeks in awe of her perfection. How Aaron wished he could heal his wife's broken heart. He didn't care that his was also broken; he just wanted her to be happy again. At the same time, he was also feeling pained from having to give up the baby. For the first time since finding out about her parent's deaths, they also cried. They were heartbroken for the orphaned baby; for the possibility of her being a child of a system who doesn't strive to provide the best life for all the children in their care. At that moment, they hoped that if they could not be her guardians, that she still had family out there somewhere.

The next morning, they were both woken up by someone knocking on their front door. Aaron got up to greet whoever it was.

"Good morning," said the detective standing on the front porch of their farmhouse.

"Good morning, Detective. What can I help you with today?"

"We found a relative of the couple," the detective said handing him a paper with the baby's parents community address.

"We have still not found the baby, however," the detective continued. It was then that Sarah stepped into his view holding the baby girl in her arms.

"This is the baby you have been looking for," Sarah said with teary eyes and a heavy heart. Sarah and Aaron were then taken to the police department in order for them to give their statement of the night that the baby was found. They were under investigation for more than a few hours but were finally released at the end of the day. There was nothing to prove that they had ever been involved with the couple's homicide and after all, they had rescued the baby from possible harm on that stormy night. The detective came out of his office holding the baby girl.

"We are going to return the baby to her community," he told them, "It's obvious that you really care about this baby. Would you like to come along?" Aaron and Sarah both nodded. They sat in the backseat of the patrol car cuddling the baby and saying their goodbyes. Upon arriving at the baby's community some 45 minutes after leaving the station, they saw that people were already waiting for her return. The detective came around to open the door for them and they stepped out. They looked at the faces of all the people praying for the baby's safe return. Both of them expected the reunion to be loud and booming with cheers and shouts of joy but it was eerily quiet. A younger woman stepped forward pushing the wheelchair of an elderly woman. Her hair was silver and she had glazed eyes.

"Anna, your great-granddaughter has been found. They have brought her back home," the young woman said to the old woman.

"I want to hold her," the woman said holding out her arms. Her voice was dry and scratchy. Sarah got closer to the woman and placed the baby in her hands. The woman brought the baby close to her face and took a deep breath. Her hands traced the baby's hands and face. She broke down and began to cry.

"Thank you, thank you," she told them both as she kissed the baby's forehead.

"We want to apologize for not returning her sooner," Aaron told her.

"We are sorry," Sarah added, "we were immediately enamored with this sweet girl of yours. We didn't want our time with her to end but she belongs with you."

"Thank you for keeping her safe," the woman told them, "Tell me, do you have other children?"

"We do not," Aaron replied, "My wife, Sarah, had complications during her pregnancy last year and we lost our first and only child. We are unable to ever become pregnant again."

"Do you want to take her back with you?" the old woman asked.

"What do you mean?" Sarah asked.

"I am very ill and don't have much time to live. I am not in the best condition to be raising a child as I am also invalid and am blind. While I do love this child with all of my heart, I cannot do much else for my great-granddaughter, Meredith."

"Are you her only relative?"

"Yes. Her mother was my granddaughter whose own mother died during childbirth. After I am gone, she will have nobody."

Sarah and Aaron stayed at the community talking with the old woman for many hours. By the time they had come to an agreement, it was already late at night so the members of the community offered them a place to stay for the night since the road was not considered safe for the time being. They learned many details of the baby's, Meredith's, family history—one that they had planned to tell her about as she grew up. As the months went by after they had returned home, they would occasionally return to visit the old woman along with baby Meredith until the old woman was no more. The woman had not lied when she said she had little to live. Although a part of their heart would always be missing from the loss of their premature child, Meredith completed their lives in unimaginable ways. Sarah had always known that she was sent by God to restore their lives. Meredith was their daughter even if not by blood. They loved her like they would have loved any child that came from their own flesh and blood. Whenever there was a thunderstorm, they were reminded of the night that Sarah gave birth to death but it also reminded them of the night that they met the most beautiful baby of all.

One True Amish Love

Erica Fanning

It was a beautiful spring day, and Lovina Miller could not have been happier. Her younger sister Sarah, walked alongside her as they admired the creation around them. This particular path through the woods behind their house brought only good memories to Lovina's mind.

"Do you remember the first time we walked this path, Sissy?" Lovina looked at her sister with a smile on her face.

"It's been awhile since you've called me that."

Sarah smiled in return. "Yeah, but you are my Sissy and sometimes... I realize I'm too hard on you."

Lovina waved her hand dismissively. "Don't you worry about it. As the oldest child, I do have more responsibility." She winked at Sarah, who simply shook her head.

They were on their way to their favorite hiding spot to meet their best friend Rachel Schwartz. The three had been inseparable practically from birth, as both sets of parents like to spin the stories. Lovina's favorite had to be the one where her parents had to pry the girls away from each other the first time they met because, even at the young ages of 4, 3, and 2, they were already the best of friends. Being in a small Plain community like theirs, there was no need for a lot of friends. Living in an agrarian society ensured their free time was limited to anytime after the sun went down and the winter months. Lovina and Sarah's father had to make sure they knew how to run everything however, because they were the only children to Josiah and Rebekah Miller; naturally one of them would inherit the farm when Josiah passed on. He seemed to think it would work better if both of them knew how to properly care for the farm, and since neither of them cared much, they concurred with his decision.

The Schwartz family, on the other hand, turned their rather large house into a small inn for a few travelers and tourists to use in the event they needed a place to stay overnight. Because of this fact, Rachel's family had to deal with some backlash from having electricity and the few amenities that came with that, but her parents were very strict about using the power and when. Mr. Schwartz made it very clear that electricity was only for the English visitors and the duration of their stay and nothing more. The business seemed to explode overnight, so Rachel seemed to be more pressed for time in the recent months.

Even though the women were now busy making their respective livings, there was one thing Lovina, Sarah, and Rachel promised they would always do no matter how busy life got or how upset they would get at each other. That one thing was to meet in the woods in their favorite clearing and simply reconnect. Sarah had made a valid point when she compared them reconnecting to why people should reconnect with God regularly: if you don't do it, your relationship will suffer. In the almost 15 years the women had been friends, they never once missed their weekly get-together.

This time seemed to be different though. Rachel was usually the late one, but Lovina and Sarah had been sitting there for almost 20 minutes and still had not heard anything. Finally, something rustled and they heard footfalls. A few seconds later, Rachel emerged from the darkness of the woods, breathless but glowing.

"Hello, sisters!" Hugs were passed around before Lovina pointed out that Rachel was glowing. "Oh, yes. Isaac Fisher has some English family in from out of town, so I was helping them get set up and then Isaac wanted to talk for a bit—"

"What did you talk about?" Sarah cut her friend off. If there was one thing the Miller sisters fought over and discussed more than any other, it was the state of Isaac Fisher and who might end up taking his hand in marriage.

"Well, I don't know..." Rachel suddenly seemed hesitant to share details as she deflated a bit. "Just normal, everyday stuff I suppose. We don't see each other very often."

"Did he talk about anyone in particular?" Lovina felt the hair on the back of her neck raise in excitement. "Other than his family of course."

"Well, no." Rachel looked her sister-friends in their faces. "I'm sorry, sisters. I know you both like him, but he seems very content to continue being single."

"Maybe, but *I'm* not content just stay single." Sarah threw her hands up. "I'm 17, Lovina's 19, and you're 18! We should be married or at least engaged at this point!"

"Now, now, Sarah," Lovina consoled her sister as they sat on a felled log and Rachel sat on the other side of Sarah.

"No, you want him just as badly as I do, Sissy! We need to figure something out before we tear each other apart." Lovina sighed and looked at Rachel.

"How old is he?"

"He's going to be 20 in June."

"Lovina," Sarah heaved a sigh. "You can't use the fact that he's closer to your age to prove that he's the man for you. Even you know age has nothing to do with it."

The heated conversation continued for a while longer and eventually Rachel slowly stopped contributing. There was no reason to keep goading one or the other sister when even she wanted to date Isaac. The truth of the matter was, Isaac had seemed to be showing more interest in Rachel as of late: coming to the Schwartz's inn at least once a week, getting to know Rachel's father, and just the day before she overheard him talking to Rachel's mother while both of them thought Rachel was upstairs out of earshot. Normally two adults having a conversation about another adult wouldn't strike Rachel as the reason that Isaac might be interested in her, but combined with the other factors, it gave Rachel a lot to think about.

When the three friends parted ways that day, Lovina and Sarah had made up by discussing the best way to determine which one of them would be better suited for Isaac Fisher and why. Rachel simply let them talk; she wasn't about to burst their bubble with something that might simply be a fantasy. She only hoped that if Isaac did have feelings for her, they were strong enough to withstand the beauty and persistence of the Miller sisters.

Weeks went by and none of the women heard from Isaac, not that it mattered much. With the summer months coming, every available adult was putting in their time and effort to make sure their respective families and the community at large had plenty to eat. This particular season had been dry for the community, so they pooled together resources to pull water from the nearby river and created an irrigation system. It was crude but it served the purpose. Although the Schwartz's inn had electricity, they chose not to have running water available since the reason many Englishers visited was to experience as much of the Plain lifestyle as possible.

It was at this point that Lovina, Sarah, and Rachel morphed their weekly get-together into time that they would gather water for their homes. The river had started to run low already and the calendar had only passed into June. There hadn't been much rain despite the fact that the whole community prayed for it. The three women decided they should keep their time focused on their families and livelihoods until the sky broke its dry spell. It was also a way for them to dispel rumors that they might be shirking their responsibilities if they all returned to their homes with at least one jar of water. On this particular day in June, Lovina and Sarah began telling Rachel of the problems they had encountered just in the past week.

"Oh Rachel, you wouldn't believe it," Lovina sighed as she pulled another precious scoop of water into the large jar that she and Sarah had brought. "Because of where we're positioned in the community, not only do we get less water, but we also get a lot more sun. Our father went to the town committee and asked them for permission to move just the garden, but they simply told him he would have to construct something to put over the plants." Rachel was quiet the whole time, and when she had finished filling her jar, she began to leave. Sarah stopped her with an observation.

"You know, you've been awfully quiet these last few weeks. And not just about the woes of your family's business, which I'm sure is doing just fine thanks to the electricity you use. I've noticed whenever we talk about Isaac Fisher, you seem to get really quiet and try all you can to leave the conversation. Why is that?"

Rachel felt her cheeks flush and was glad she was facing the other direction. She composed herself to the best of her abilities, turned to face her best friends, and replied, "Because honestly, I'm interested in him too. I can't keep it from you two, but at the same time you both want him. I just want us all to have a fair chance at this guy, but obsessing over him isn't going to help anything. Especially now that our community is in danger because of the lack of rain." She paused for a breath before continuing. "If we're all really honest with ourselves, would our relationship ever be the same if Isaac Fisher picked one of us? I think we would be better off if Isaac Fisher picked *none* of us. So yes, I have been quiet lately. There are a lot of things to think about... and I don't want to take one thing more lightly than another." Before the sisters could say anything more, Rachel picked up her jar of water and left. She had said all she was going to for one day. She just prayed their relationship would be able to withstand any and all obstacles pertaining to men.

After Rachel left, Lovina and Sarah continued talking.

"I think Rachel and Isaac already have a thing," Sarah conjectured.

"Maybe," Lovina conceded. "But would that be such a bad thing? It might be better if neither of us date Isaac and we simply pass him off to the next highest bidder... so to speak."

"First, I don't appreciate the fact that you just made it sound like we were at an auction, trying to be sold off. Second, I have never known you to be a quitter, even in the matter of men." With Sarah's jar finally filled, she stood upright and placed a hand on her hip. "I don't understand why you just don't say something to her."

"Why would I need to be the one to say something? She's your friend too!"

"But she listens to you, Sissy! That's why I would prefer that you talk to her." Lovina scoffed as she placed her jar on her shoulders. Sarah followed suit.

"Look Sarah, even if Rachel does have some attraction to Isaac, she's done an amazing job of hiding it. Why don't we just decide who's actually going to date the man and carry on with our lives?" Sarah sighed.

"I hope you're right about Rachel not being into him."

Home was still out of sight when they noticed that the air was thick with smoke. They looked at each with a note of worry and picked up their pace. When they arrived at their house, the first thing they saw was the fire just on the edge of their property and Josiah was trying desperately to stop it from crossing the line. Lovina ran over to Josiah.

"How can I help?" Josiah looked at her, worry etched into his face.

"Grab a few essential items from the house, collect your mother and sister and get out of here!"

"I won't leave you!"

But Josiah was hearing none of it. "There's not much we can do to stop it, but I can hold it off until everyone is safe."

"Promise me you'll get out of the danger zone as soon as you can." Josiah looked at Lovina a moment and nodded.

"I love you, my child." They embraced only a moment before Lovina ran inside to help her mom and sister pack.

Within minutes, people from all over town were coming by to help quell the fire, but it was too late. It had begun to take over the Miller's farmland. The men fought the fire to keep it from reaching the house, but a gust of wind picked up. Soon, embers turned into flames and began to lick at the wood in the house. By the time any Englisher firefighters showed up, the Millers no longer had a home or any kind of livelihood.

Rachel showed up and invited them to stay at the inn for as long as they needed. The Schwartzes put them in the largest bedroom they had. They still needed to make money and the Millers were grateful for any help they could get.

Rachel normally wasn't the type of girl to take advantage of a bad situation, but when it came to Isaac Fisher, she wasn't opposed to doing some crazy things. It didn't help that both of her parents wholeheartedly approved of him and told her as much any chance they could. Lovina and Sarah didn't spend a lot of time at the inn because they were finding work in different areas of the community. Thanks to Josiah, their skill set was different than most women so they had a harder time doing the jobs that most women actually did to raise funds. Since they were gone a lot and Isaac would come visit while they were gone, Rachel was able to spend more and more time with her long-time "crush"... as the Englishers would call it.

However, Isaac wasn't there to see her on this particular day, for this day was his birthday. No, Isaac Fisher wanted to invite everyone in the community to his birthday celebration.

"I have something special planned for everyone tonight," he announced at the inn, just as he had announced in the town square earlier. "We have been through so much as a community. It's time that we stand together and show the world what we're made of. There will be festivities tonight at the church at sundown. Please try to be prompt." He held Rachel's gaze for an extra beat before heading out the door to make the announcement wherever else it might need to be made.

There were a few Englishers staying at the inn and even they were intrigued as to what might occur at this special birthday party. No one was more excited about what might be happening than Rachel's own mother. Lovina and Sarah noticed it when they returned from the field that evening.

"Did you hear Isaac Fisher's announcement?" Rachel asked after realizing how crazy her mother might seem to them. They both shook their heads. "Well, he's having a birthday celebration tonight and says he wants to try to give back to the community in some way. Mama is really excited because," Rachel looked at her mother and lowered her voice to a whisper, "she thinks Isaac is going to ask to court me tonight."

At first the sisters seemed concerned until eventually Lovina started laughing, then Sarah. Pretty soon, even Rachel's mother was laughing and she had no idea why.

"Aww, it's so nice to see the three of you, still as inseparable as ever." Mrs. Schwartz gave the three of them a hug before forcing them to wash up and prepare for the special evening at the church.

When the friends arrived at the party less than an hour later, things already seemed to be in full swing.

"We're not... late, are we?" Sarah asked, unsure of what was going on.

"Even if we are, he specifically said 6." Rachel would never have a hard time remembering anything Isaac told her, she was sure of that.

"Ah! If it isn't the three people I wanted to see!" Rachel spun at the voice, but instantly knew it belonged to Isaac. "You all look lovely tonight." He kissed each of their hands, but seemed to hold Rachel's a second longer, or so it seemed. Lovina and Sarah must have noticed it as well because they gave Rachel a dirty look. Isaac took no notice of the civil war about to ensue; he simply ushered them all to a place of prominence at the head table and clapped his hands to get everyone's attention.

"Listen up, everybody! Our guests of honor have arrived, and tonight is all about them. First of all, let's welcome Lovina and Sarah Miller." Cheers and applause came from everywhere. "These hard working, young women don't care what it takes to make sure their family is provided for. I'm not sure how many of you are aware of this, but these young women have been working out in the fields for hire since their field and house burned by the fire two weeks ago. Tonight, I wanted to take a few moments and honor them... as well as give them some of what I have to help their family get back on their feet."

He handed them a small box, but Rachel already suspected they would find money in there. Lovina took the box and opened it since Sarah seemed to be in too much shock to do anything. Lovina slowly undid the bow at the top and removed the lid. She saw what was in there, and went to reach for it before Isaac stopped her. He whispered something in her ear and she gasped as tears filled her eyes.

"Thank you" was all she managed to get out.

"Let the record show," Isaac said with a dramatic flare. "That I gifted her with a rather large amount of money. Seeing as how she and her family have had problems, I did what I know to do to help out." There was more cheering and applause before he quieted the crowd again.

"And here, ever by their side, is the beautiful Rachel Schwartz. We all know the story; they practically had the same mother." There was some laughter. Rachel was unsure of what Isaac was doing, but she smiled and played along. "For all the years of faithfulness, of being by their side, and of showing me what true love really looks like..." Isaac pulled a small box out of his pocket and got down next to Rachel on one knee. "Thank you." He opened the box to reveal a small locket. Rachel gasped, but looked at Isaac confused.

"You're not usually one for the dramatic," she whispered, though just about everyone in the clearing could hear her. Isaac smiled and shrugged.

"You make me do crazy things." Then he stood, pulled the locket out and placed it around her neck. "Let the record show that I gave Rachel Miller my great-grandmother's locket because I believe she's worth it..." he looked at Rachel. "And my grandmother would be proud that I have chosen you."

Rachel couldn't breathe. Did Isaac really just say that? Was this his way of asking her out? Why didn't he just ask? She couldn't just say yes! What about Lovina and Sarah? She suddenly felt light-headed as she forced herself to look at her friends. What she saw would have made any other girl rip the locket off and run away forever.

Lovina and Sarah both looked as though they were hurt and upset about the fact that Rachel didn't simply come to them sooner. Rachel had spent her entire life with them, naturally they would understand, but instead she had told them that she would stand aside while they tried to vye for Isaac Fisher's affection.

"I guess everything you said that day really was a lie," Sarah spat and removed herself with as much dignity as was possible. Isaac had been talking up to that point, but none of them heard what he had said and it wasn't until Sarah left that Isaac realized something was amiss.

"Uh, let the party resume!" He quickly threw everyone back into the celebration, and Rachel was glad that all eyes were no longer on her. She had yet to actually inspect the locket, but she didn't want to come to terms with the fact that Isaac chose her and no one else. Looking at the locket would make it all too real. Lovina moved closer to Rachel.

"Why didn't you tell us this would happen?" Rachel looked at her best friend.

"You think I knew about this? Trust me, if I knew this would happen—"

"I'm not talking about the party, Rachel!" Lovina hissed through her teeth. "I'm talking about your affections for Isaac and his for you! You had to have known *that* was going to happen!" She slid out of her seat and followed her sister into the night, leaving Rachel feeling more alone and more scared than she had ever felt.

"What was that all about?" Isaac queried as he watched Lovina leave.

"Sometimes life doesn't go the way people expect it to. For once, it worked out in my favor, but my friends simply aren't happy for me."

"Then they're not really friends." Rachel spun her head toward Isaac.

"They are my *best friends*."

"I don't doubt that, but why are they your best friends? Because you've never had any other close friends? Because they've proven time and again that they're for you? Or because you all have the same life story and you might as well be actual sisters?"

Rachel was starting to see where Isaac was going, but she didn't like the direction.

"Can we not talk about them as if they're abusive?"

"Aren't they? Rachel, I'm not dumb. I know you've had an interest in me for a long time. It wasn't until very recently that the Miller sisters started to show some interest in me as well. I watched you continuously reject my advances because you knew that they were into me. Would that have gone differently if you didn't know? Or better yet, if they were really, truly friends?"

"God's Word says, 'Greater love hath no man than this—'"

Isaac stopped her. "I know what the Bible says. I'm not asking the Bible, I'm asking *you*." Rachel looked at him for a long moment.

"The reason I did what I did was because I love them, and I want them to be happy. If you can't see that, then maybe you're the one who needs to reevaluate your friends."

Before Isaac had a chance to respond, Rachel stormed off in the same direction as her friends, half in hopes that she could find them to apologize and half in hopes that she didn't. She wasn't sure her heart could take anymore surprises. The only place she knew to go where she wouldn't be bothered was the secret get-together place. The sun had gone down over an hour before, but that didn't stop Rachel. On more than one occasion she had to make that trip in the dark, and it came back to her with ease on this particular night. She heard sniffles as she approached the clearing, but knew she had made enough noise that they already knew she was coming.

"Go away!"

Yep, they heard me alright, she thought to herself.

"I just want to talk."

"What is there to talk about? Isaac *clearly* loves you more than me or Sarah. What's the point of even trying?"

Rachel had stopped short of the clearing. In the small amount of moonlight, she could just make out the silhouettes of Lovina and Sarah. The youngest was resting her head in her sister's lap while the oldest looked as though she was waiting to start stoning Rachel. The only difference was she didn't actually have any stones to throw, and Rachel was glad for that.

"Look, there's no way to undo what was done—"

"You're right. There's not!" Sarah sat up and seemed to see straight through the darkness. She made eye contact with Rachel. "Clearly Isaac has chosen you, so now you have to make a choice. Us or him?"

"What? How can I make that kind of—"

"It doesn't matter," Lovina stated flatly. "We need you to either break up with him or never see us again."

"Well that's kind of hard to do when you currently live with me."

"Oh, you'll see us... but this will be the last time we ever talk to you, talk about you, or talk for you. We will no longer be your friends. So make your decision. You have 24 hours."

"24 hours!" Rachel moved into the clearing. "You can't do that! At least give me three days!" Lovina and Sarah looked at each other and smiled.

"There's the Rachel we know and love," Sarah stood and spanned the small clearing in two steps. "We will give you three days, but only because you asked for it. Choose wisely. Your future is determined by who you marry, you know."

"Now get out of here. We prefer you went to bed first tonight. We have some talking to do."

Rachel spun on her heel, feeling as though she had been played. Unfortunately she had no evidence to support the theory, so she continued walking until she reached home. As soon as she made it to her bedroom she closed the door, locked it, and wept bitterly.

Back at the clearing, Lovina and Sarah were entrenched in conversation.

"Can you believe the nerve of that woman? I can't believe we called her our friend!" Sarah was livid and would find any excuse to murder something... which she did by destroying the ends of the log that the friends would sit on for reprieve.

"Do you really have to be so violent to get your point across?" Lovina asked as she continued to sit on the log.

"Why do you always have to be the one that has everything figured out? Why can't you just be upset for once?"

"I am upset," Lovina replied quietly. "But I'm more upset that we might be missing out on one of the greatest adventures of Rachel's life... and we're bringing her down just because we don't agree with what happened. This isn't us, Sarah. We're adults for crying out loud!"

"No," Sarah retorted. "Rachel is just as much responsible for her actions as we are. Why didn't she tell us? She could have redirected us so many times!"

"But she didn't." Lovina stood. "Sarah, I think Rachel didn't say anything for a reason. I think she really wanted to give us a fair shot at dating Isaac."

"I feel like they've both liked each other for as long as I can tell."

"Well, I don't know about him, but I know she has been crazy for him for a long time... but she said she had gotten over it." Lovina was pacing now, and thinking of different possibilities. "Maybe she was just being the good friend that we've always been told she should be."

Sarah threw up her arms. "Well we've been doing a poor job of that then, haven't we?"

Lovina nodded, still thinking. "Come on, let's go get some sleep. We can talk about this tomorrow."

Rachel woke up more tired than when she fell asleep. In fact, she didn't even remember falling asleep. The weight of sadness pushed on her chest, making it hard to breathe. Last night could have been the best and worst night of her life. What good would it be to have a husband but lose your friends? Or what good would it be to have friends, but remain single for the rest of your life?

These are the questions that plagued Rachel's mind before she even made it to the washroom that morning. She ran into Lovina in the hallway, but she was already dressed.

"What time is it?" Rachel asked groggily.

"The sun has been up for a few hours... are you okay?" Lovina's face twisted into concern for her friend.

"I'm fine. I was just given the ultimatum to give up one future for another." Rachel tried very hard to rein her tongue in, but once she started she found the words flowed extremely easily. "Because I can't have a husband without my best friends, but my best friends want the only man that I've ever really loved. I did what I thought was right, but all it did was get me into this mess where now it seems as though everyone hates me." Tears were flowing down both women's faces as Sarah emerged from the Miller's room.

"No, Rachel. We don't hate you. We love you, and we want what's best for you." All three of them were now standing in the hallway. Sarah continued, "I acted very poorly last night and I'm sorry. It was never my intention to pull you away from what makes you happy... it was just... so hard for me to accept the fact that we all happened to like the same man." She chuckled wryly. "Our entire livelihood burning down didn't help any."

Lovina and Rachel both smiled at that and Lovina concurred. "We love you, sister. You've had your eye on Isaac since first grade; we're not going to take that away from you now."

Sarah added, "And you don't have to give one up for the other. Lovina and I had a long talk last night and we realized... I was kind of being hard on you. We were so sure that one of us would end up courting him, and then you showed up almost out of nowhere and steal him away." She laughed. "But life doesn't always work out the way we plan."

"No, I should be sorry," Rachel began. "I should have told you guys that I never really got over Isaac or that he had started to show interest in me. I mean, we're sisters after all. I should be willing to share everything with you! But when you both started talking about him like you were interested, I didn't want to disappoint you. I was even willing to step away if one of you could actually win his heart."

"Is that why you all ran away last night?"

The three friends jumped and spun at the new voice. There was Isaac Fisher, standing at the top of the stairs, arms folded with a smirk on his face.

"Isaac!" Rachel exclaimed. "How long have you been there?" He laughed.

"Long enough to know that you three really need to work on your communication skills. Though I do admire your willingness to admit when you're wrong and the way you are *now* fixing the problem." The women looked at each other and giggled.

"You know, I've actually known for a while that you all were interested in me. I'm not naive. In fact, I would be lying if I said you were the *only three* interested in me in this entire community." He gave them a knowing look and more giggles ensued.

"Why did I pick Rachel? Why did I do it the way I did? Because I wanted you all to know that I knew what was going on. I wanted you all to know what was going on, and since it was my 20th birthday, I figured why not. Also, I did want to help out the Miller family since your family has been a huge help to this community. It's only right that the community should not only be made aware of the situation, but also work on doing better at taking care of our people."

He continued, "All three of you are extremely beautiful women and any man who isn't smart enough to see that it's not just an outward beauty isn't deserving of your love. But Rachel has won my heart with her soft voice and caring heart." He looked around at the hallway and lowered his voice. "Because anyone who can deal with a noisy Englisher is definitely a winner in my book."

It had been three months since Isaac confronted Lovina, Sarah, and Rachel in the hallway of the Schwartz family inn. The community had in fact come together to help the Miller family with gifts of money, time, and love. In the short months since the fire, the community had managed to build a new house for the Millers and they were able to move in before the weather started to get too cold. Since it was almost harvest time, the family were to be paid in the food that the Miller sisters helped to harvest as well as extra dishes and fruits and vegetables that the community pooled together to supply for them.

As for Isaac and Rachel, their relationship blossomed much faster than most in the community thought it would. What they didn't know was that the community's newest couple had been working on their relationship long before they were ever considered to be dating. Lovina and Sarah were the only people outside of the Schwartz and Fisher families that really knew the depth of Rachel and Isaac's relationship.

The three friends continued their weekly get-togethers, but after a while, they began including Isaac too. He was certainly not a lady, but he was now accepted as part of the family.

"I'm glad Lovina and Sarah let me hang out with you ladies," he mentioned on their short walk back to Rachel's house.

"Me too. It was nice to see that they can be adults sometimes. It's funny, that even without a lot of *Rumspringa* going on, we still feel as though we're not fully adults. It's like we forget just how old we really are."

"Yes, the next generation and the like." Rachel raised an eyebrow at him.

"'And the like'?" Isaac laughed.

"I guess that's something I used to hear a lot. 'Gotta be a good example for the next generation!' I just added the 'like.'" Rachel now laughed.

"Wow, you're so smart, Mr. Fisher. Maybe I should reconsider my stance with you."

"On that note," suddenly Isaac dropped to one knee. She heard rustling coming from the woods, but ignored it. Was that her parents coming from the house? She never took her eyes off of Isaac because she was afraid she might miss the most important moment in her life. "Rachel Grace Schwartz, I have asked for your father's blessing to have your hand in marriage. I love you, and always have loved you, since the day we met. Would you do the honor of making me your husband?"

Rachel was so touched by the way he said everything, she couldn't even get the word "yes" out, so she nodded excitedly. Tears fell from her eyes faster than she could register that they were falling. She couldn't see what Isaac was holding, but it looked like another small jewelry box.

"Put it on," she finally managed. As soon as she felt the ring slip on her finger, she threw her arms around her one true love and whispered into his ear. "I love you, my darling. And I will never let you go."

He pulled her back long enough to look into her teary eyes and he kissed her hard on the lips. "I promised myself I wouldn't do that," he mentioned after they broke away from each other.

"If you hadn't, I would have," she half-laughed, half-cried.

Suddenly, as if they were pushed in front of a waiting mass of people, sound seemed to explode around them and everything came back into focus. People were cheering, some were crying, many were coming over and giving slaps on the back to Isaac and hugs to Rachel. This really was a dream come true.